THE CHESSBOARD SPIES

A man is murdered in a street in Istanbul and as a result of his death, Stephen Fletcher, alias Sefan Fettos, a British agent, and David Maxwell, a C.I.A. agent, become involved in a spy game on the chessboard of the Middle East. In their bid to foil a Russian threat they move first to Cairo, then to Athens, and finally into the remote province of Eastern Turkey. En route, Fletcher comes across Mustafa Kaddir who is purchasing illegal arms, he also becomes suspicious of a party of American officials. This is a chilling tale filled with the atmosphere of these turbulent countries.

THE CHESSBOARD SPIES

The Chessboard Spies

by

Geoffrey Davison

Magna Large Print Books
Long Preston, North Yorkshire,
BD23 4ND, England.

British Library Cataloguing in Publication Data.

Davison, Geoffrey
     The chessboard spies.

     A catalogue record of this book is
     available from the British Library

     ISBN   978-0-7505-3662-2

First published in Great Britain in 1974 by Robert Hale & Co.

Copyright © Geoffrey Davison 1974

Cover illustration © Collaboration JS/Arcangel Images

The moral right of the author has been asserted

A catalogue record for this book is available from the British Library

Published in Large Print 2013 by arrangement with
Geoffrey Davison, care of Watson, Little Ltd.

Magna Large Print is an imprint of Library Magna Books Ltd.

Printed and bound in Great Britain by
T.J. (International) Ltd., Cornwall, PL28 8RW

To

Nigel

Chapter One

The two men in the car sat silently staring out of the window along the dark, dimly lit street, where the street lamps cast shrouded lights in the rain soaked atmosphere. It was a broad, cobbled street, in Istanbul. Along one side ran a narrow pavement with large, overhanging trees, from the adjoining park. On the other side was the high brick wall of an army barracks, built in the reign of Kemal Ataturk.

The two men were both dressed alike in dark, navy gaberdine raincoats, and dark trilby hats, but the man in the passenger seat was much taller than his companion. He sat upright, stone faced, giving no indication of the anticipation that he felt. His companion was less relaxed. He glanced at the fingers on his illuminated wrist watch. It was past ten p.m.

'He's late,' he whispered.

The other man didn't answer him; he had seen something in the distance.

'Here he is,' he muttered.

The man behind the steering wheel leant forward and saw a hunched figure appear out of the darkness. He sat back and waited. As the figure came closer, the tall man pulled up the collar of his raincoat and moved to open the car door.

'Wait,' the other man hissed hurriedly. 'There is something the matter. He is not stopping!' He switched on the windscreen wipers. The other man held back and watched the hunched figure walk past on the opposite side of the road.

'What the devil is he up to?' he asked urgently.

'He is being followed,' the other man whispered.

The tall man glanced along the road again and saw another figure hurrying towards them. The figure started to run. As he came alongside them, the two men in the car saw something flash in his hand.

'My God!' the tall man yelled. 'Quick! We have to stop him.'

Desperately the two men flung open their doors and ran onto the road. The man who had been running along the pavement had caught up with the first man. As the two men from the car crossed the roadway, a loud, piercing cry, came from the two figures, and one slumped to the ground. The other figure started to run away. One of the men from the car – the smaller one – stopped in his tracks and withdrew a revolver. He steadied himself and shot twice at the moving figure. It fell to the ground, but they were too late.

The first man had a long stiletto sticking in his back!

The tall man leant over the body and quickly withdrew the dagger.

'Get the car,' he shouted. The other man didn't hesitate. In the barracks a number of lights had appeared and shouts could be heard. The tall man gently lifted the body into his arms. He could feel a warm trickle of blood over his hand, but there was still life in the body – very little, but it was there. Frantically the other man swung the car around and drew up to where the tall man was standing. The tall man calmly placed the body in the rear seat. He could hear more shouts coming from the barracks. They would have to get clear of the area, but first he wanted to look at the assassin. He ran up to the still form lying face downwards with two small holes below the neck. He turned the body over and shone his torch on the dead man's face. It was a lean, thin face, with a hooked nose and fair hair. It was an unusual face, the man thought. It didn't look Turkish. It looked more Arabic!

The man in the car raced the engine impatiently, and the tall man quickly joined him. As he did so, a pair of headlamps appeared from the entrance to the barracks. The man behind the steering wheel slammed in the gears and shot away into the darkness.

'Where to?' he asked.

His companion gave him an address in the old quarter of Istanbul. The driver nodded his head, understandingly, and swung into a side street and headed for the Galata Bridge. He didn't reduce his speed until they had crossed the bridge and were hidden in the maze of narrow, deserted streets. They came to the address the other man had given him – an old terraced building close to the Blue Mosque, and parked the car in a darkened alley way.

The tall man gently lifted the body out of the rear seat whilst the other man knocked on the door. Presently, the door opened and an old woman appeared. She looked first at the figure in the man's arms and then into the face of the man carrying the body. Their eyes met, but she said nothing. Silently she opened the door to its full extent and stood to one side. The tall man entered the building and carried the body up a steep flight of steps. Before he had reached the top of the staircase, the entrance door had been shut and bolted behind him, and standing waiting for him on the first floor landing was the woman's husband – a small man like his wife, with a stubbly grey beard and a pair of dark brown eyes, which watched the man's progress from behind thick lensed spectacles. He was a Turk, and had once been a doctor, until his politics had fallen foul of the authorities. He turned and opened a side door.

'In here,' he said.

The man carrying the body followed him into the room. It was the kitchen. The Turk quickly cleared the table and pulled it under the central electric light bulb. The tall man laid the body on the table and stood back as the Turk started his examination.

Whatever happened, the tall man thought, the man on the table was going to die. There was no hope for him. But first he had to talk.

The Turk came up to him.

'There is nothing I can do for him,' he whispered. 'Perhaps a hospital could save him, but I have nothing.'

The tall man looked straight into the Turk's dark brown eyes, and unflinchingly said: 'Nobody can save him. He has to die. But first he must talk.'

The Turk shrugged.

'He must,' the man pleaded. For the first time there was a note of urgency in his voice. The Turk looked at him again.

'It is essential,' the man said. The Turk read the determination on his face.

'Go into the other room,' he said quietly. 'I will call you if it is to be.'

The man left the kitchen and went into the adjoining room, where his companion and the old lady were sitting. As he joined them, the old lady stood up and left the room. The other man, who was also a Turk, lit a black, strongly scented cigarette, and relaxed in his chair, unconcerned whether the body on the kitchen table lived or died. The tall man glanced around the room at the dark, ornate wallpaper and old fashioned furniture, and closed his eyes. He was a man in his early thirties, with a strong, tanned face, black hair, and steel blue eyes which belied his toughness. For like his companion, he was a man who had become hardened to the unsavoury dealings of the underworld. But he was not a Turk.

Presently, the old lady returned with a tray of strong coffee. She handed the two men each a cup of the beverage and returned to her seat, and became engrossed in her needlework. The tall man mumbled his thanks, but didn't engage her in conversation. He was imposing on a past friendship in bringing the dying man to their house; the least they knew about it, the better it would be for them.

When the old Turk joined them, the look on his face told the tall man that his chances of getting anything out of their patient were slim.

'You can try,' the Turk said, 'but he is sinking fast.'

The tall man rushed into the temporary surgery. The body was still on the table, his head resting on a pillow, and his chest thickly bandaged.

The man went up to him. He had seen many dying men before, but this one looked more pathetic. His face was pale and drawn, his features more pronounced, his nostrils broad, and his eyebrows thick and untidy. It was a sad face, the tall man thought, sad and troubled. A face which had hidden the battle which had gone on in the man's mind. A battle between conscience and loyalty. A battle in which conscience had won, but for which the man must die.

The tall man leant over the figure on the table.

'Andre,' he whispered, 'Andre.'

The eyes of the man on the table opened and closed. The tall man called out his name again, this time more sharply.

The eyes opened, blinked, and closed again.

'Andre,' the man said. 'You are going to be all right, but you must give me your message.' He had spoken in Russian using the dying man's native tongue. 'Give me your message,' he said again, close to the dying man's ear.

The Russian's eyes opened, looked into the tall man's face and closed again. But his lips started to move.

The man leant forward, his ear close to the Russian's mouth.

'Brez … Brez…' the Russian whispered.

'Brez what?' the man asked urgently. 'Breznov?'

The Russian lay still.

'Breznov!' the man shouted. 'Andre! Was it Breznov?'

The voice penetrated the Russian's dulled brain. His eyes opened wide.

'Breznov?' the man repeated the name.

Again the Russian's lips moved. The man leant forward and listened.

'Brez … Brez … nov…'

'What about him Andre? What about Breznov?'

The Russian opened his mouth and tried to struggle forward.

'K … k … k … ka … kad … kad.'

He slumped back on the table.

'Kad what?' the man called out. 'Kad what?'

A shrill, guttural rattle, came from the Russian's throat. The tall man stood up. The Russian could say no more; he was dead! The man sighed, and closed the dead man's eyes and folded his arms over his chest. When he looked up he was surprised to see the old Turk standing close by. There was a look of concern on his face.

'You heard?' the man asked.

The Turk indicated that he had.

'There will be repercussions,' he whispered seriously.

The man shook his head.

16

'Don't worry, it will pass. They killed him themselves. So long as they find out that he is dead, they will be satisfied.'

'Where will you take him?'

The man thought for a while.

'Somewhere close to where we found him,' he said quietly, almost with reverence. 'In that way it will look as if we picked him up, found that he was dead, and then got rid of him.'

'I went through his jacket while you were speaking to him. This is all he had.'

He handed the tall man a small amount of Turkish currency, a bunch of keys, and a newspaper cutting. The man read the newspaper cutting with interest. On one side was a list of the stock market prices of certain local and international firms. The Russian had supposedly been part of a trade mission, his business in Istanbul being to promote trade with the Soviet Union. Several of the names listed on the cutting had been underlined. Two were international firms of repute, the others were local industries. The cutting had been torn at the bottom across one of the names the Russian had underlined, as if it had been torn out of a newspaper in haste. The man mentally sighed. At least they had got something out of the meeting. The names of the firms would be of interest to his Government. He glanced at the reverse side of the cutting. Two news items were reported. One announced the arrival in Baghdad of Dr Bradshaw and a team of officials of the American Peace Corps. The other, torn at the bottom, was of a shipping order won by an Italian firm to build a two hundred and eighty thousand ton oil tanker.

The man placed the cutting in his pockets along with the keys, and started to go through the dead man's clothing with meticulous care. Even the seams of his jacket were opened and examined. But it was a fruitless search and the man gained no further information. He then set about removing the bandages from the dead body and other signs of medical attention, and with the help of the Turk he dressed the corpse.

'Will you tell Kumel?' he asked the Turk quietly.

The Turk left the room and the man placed some money on the table and picked up the dead body. At the head of the flight of stairs, he hesitated and glanced into the adjoining room where the old lady was silently doing her needlework. She felt his eyes upon her and looked at him. Their eyes met. The man gave a faint smile. The old lady smiled back, but a worried expression came over her face. She saw a hardness and determination in the man's strong face and it troubled her. She had seen it before in her husband's face and she knew the suffering it had brought them. She dropped her eyes and returned to her needlework. The man turned and carried the body down the flight of steps.

They placed the body in the boot of the car, and drove back across the Galata Bridge to the area in which they had picked up the Russian. In a deserted corner of the park they dumped the body and hurriedly returned to the sanctuary of the old quarter, where the two men parted company. The tall man got out of the car and the other man drove off into the rain swept night.

The tall man turned up the collar of his raincoat, and with his hands in his pockets, set off at a brisk pace through the myriad of narrow streets. He moved silently and unobtrusively through the almost deserted alleyways, keeping to the shadows and avoiding the many pools which had formed in the uneven surface. But as he walked he kept a watchful eye that he was not being followed, and his hand in his pocket gripped an automatic in case of any sudden encounter. For the man was a spy – a British spy – a paid agent of the British Government, and in Istanbul, as in any other part of the Balkans or Middle East, the undercurrents between the two powers on either side of the Iron Curtain, became issues in which their agents fought with any weapon, and the score was not kept.

The man's name was Stephen Fletcher, alias Stefan Fettos, and although his face didn't reflect any emotion, he inwardly felt a burning anger at losing the Russian. The old woman's diagnosis had not been wrong. It was becoming a personal issue with him. The Russians had scored a victory over him, and he would not rest until he had evened the score.

Fletcher was no stranger to Istanbul, although his normal centre of operations was Piraeus and Athens. His movements depended upon where the play was being made. At the moment it was in Istanbul, but in the turbulent countries at the eastern end of the Mediterranean it could move from country to country like a bouncing rubber ball. It was a part of the world where political intrigues and subterfuges bubbled to the surface like the rumblings of a bad tempered volcano. On occasions the volcano erupted and overflowed its fiery lava, like the Turko-Greek dispute over Cyprus, or the more violent conflict between the Arabs and the Israelis. On such occasions Britain's Secret Service worked overtime. Fortunately their influence in the area is well established and well informed. This had been proved during the Arab-Israeli war when the combined British and American Intelligence Services were shown to be far superior than their Soviet counterpart. But in a never ending battle the pendulum swings from side to side. At the critical moment during the Arab war the pendulum was with the West, but since that time it had gradually swung back into the Soviets' corner. In the past six months the West had suffered several setbacks, the Americans more so that the British. In addition to a number of highly damaging information leaks, there had also been a number of assassinations. Good Western agents and well placed supporters of the West mysteriously eliminated. Somehow the Russians had got the upper hand, and one of Fletcher's jobs was to help to restore the pendulum to its former position. He didn't work alone, nor did he work entirely on his own initiative. He was part of an organisation controlled by the Director of British Intelligence for the Balkans, Colonel John Spencer, the man Fletcher was hurrying through the darkened streets to meet. It had been Spencer who had put Fletcher on to the Russian, Andre Timovsky, and who had watched from the background whilst Fletcher had nurtured the Russian, like a prize gardener nurtured his latest creation until it was ready for picking. Timovsky had not been a newcomer to the game. He had lost his virginity over a year ago when he had become an informer to the American C.I.A. in Ankara. But a sudden relapse of conscience had caused a temporary barrier and the Americans had wisely lain off him, knowing they could force his hand at any time they needed.

Timovsky had been sent back to Moscow and had become a back number, until he had turned up suddenly, two months previous, on a trade delegation to Istanbul. He had been immediately approached again, not by the C.I.A., but by British Intelligence, and with success. A number of secret meetings had taken place between Timovsky and Fletcher and the Russian's confidence had been established. Their last meeting had promised to be the pay off. A secret directive from the K.G.B. headquarters in the Kremlin had been passed to all their Ambassadors in the Middle East. It was a statement of fact and future policy. Timovsky had learned of its contents and had intended to pass the information over to Fletcher at their next meeting. Fletcher, Spencer, and the masterminds of British Intelligence in London had been waiting for such a moment. Their wait and patience had been in vain.

It didn't take Fletcher long to reach the place he had to report to – a shuttered café in one of the many bazaars. Inside waiting for him at one of the tables, in the otherwise deserted room, were two men. One was a small, portly, military looking man, wearing a crumpled fawn suit. He sat with a large white handkerchief in his hand ready to mop his perspiring bald head. He was Colonel John Spencer, the man Fletcher worked for. The other man was of medium build, with close cropped, grey hair, and a rough tanned face. He was a man in his late fifties. A hard, tough man, who asked for no quarter and gave none. A man who matched Fletcher with his dedication, and a man for whom Fletcher had a lot of respect. His name was Maxwell – David Edward Maxwell. He was an American, born and bred in Chicago, but for the past twenty years had worked for the American C.I.A. in the Middle East. He was Spencer's counterpart, but there the similarity ended. Spencer was a backroom operator, whereas Maxwell's forthright manner demanded that he became more actively involved.

Fletcher took off his raincoat and joined the two men. They looked up at him eagerly as he sat and faced them. Spencer, however, was less impatient than Maxwell. He passed a bottle and a glass over to him, and said gruffly, 'Help yourself.'

Maxwell said: 'What kept you?'

Fletcher came straight to the point.

'Timovsky is dead,' he said pouring himself a drink.

Spencer froze in the act of raising his glass and scowled.

'My God!' Maxwell cried. 'What happened?'

'He was murdered,' Fletcher explained. 'With this.'

He threw the stiletto on to the table. He

had examined it earlier. There was nothing special about it. It was like many which could be purchased locally.

Maxwell picked up the weapon and stuck it forcibly into the table top.

'Blast!' he fumed. 'Of all the damnable bad luck.'

Fletcher appreciated his disappointment; the C.I.A. had suffered a number of setbacks.

Spencer slowly sank his drink.

'Let's have the details,' he growled.

Fletcher gave him the facts as they had taken place.

'The assassin?' Spencer asked when he had finished. 'Was he one of their own men?'

'No,' Fletcher replied. 'He didn't look Turkish, neither. More Arabic.'

'Arabic!' Spencer frowned. 'Odd.'

'Did you get anything out of him before he died?' Maxwell asked.

'Yes. He mentioned a name – Breznov.'

'Breznov!' Spencer said and looked impressed.

Maxwell gave an appreciative whistle. 'One of the K.G.B. hierarchy,' he drawled.

'We got a report of his movements,' Spencer said, but didn't say where it had come from. 'He is due in Cairo tomorrow.'

'Cairo!' Maxwell exchanged sharp glances with Spencer.

'Anything else?' Spencer asked.

'He muttered another name. It began with

K, but he was so incoherent that it could have been anything.'

The three men sat silently trying to solve the riddle the Russian had left them with, but without success.

'I also found this in his pocket.' Fletcher handed over the newspaper cutting to Spencer, who examined it and passed it to Maxwell.

'Interesting,' Maxwell said more cheerfully. 'The State Department will be pleased to get a list of these firms.'

'So will several others,' Spencer added.

Maxwell handed the cutting back to Spencer.

'You'll let me have a copy?' he asked.

Spencer nodded his head.

'And a bunch of keys,' Fletcher sighed. 'That's the lot.'

The two men examined the keys, but made no comment.

'What's the next move?' Maxwell asked sternly.

Spencer wiped the perspiration from his brow. It was an action he did to give himself time to think. He then charged his glass and passed the bottle to Maxwell who filled the two remaining glasses.

'The Soviets are up to something,' he said barely above a whisper. 'Everything points to it. They lost face during the Israeli-Arab war so they will have to redeem themselves. Their intelligence has the edge at the moment, so if they don't act soon they might lose their advantage. Any day now they are going to drop a bombshell into the laps of our diplomats.' He paused to have a drink. Fletcher waited patiently, but Maxwell lit a cigarette and inhaled deeply. Fletcher sensed a feeling of anxiety about the man. The State Department were cutting up rough, he thought.

'Timovsky informs us of this directive from the Kremlin,' Spencer continued. 'According to the message we got from him, it is something big – very big. So big in fact that they make damn sure he didn't live to tell anyone about it. But in his last breaths he mentioned a name – Breznov. Now we all know Breznov's duties. Besides being a member of their Foreign Office, he is also the link man with the KG.B. We also know he is due in Cairo tomorrow for talks with the Egyptian F.O.' He clenched his fist. 'He is our key man. We must find out what he is up to and then we might see daylight.' He wiped his forehead again.

Maxwell pressed his cigarette into the ashtray.

'How are you placed in Cairo?' he asked.

'Fair,' Spencer growled. 'We have to watch our step, but we can get by.'

'You're lucky,' Maxwell sighed. 'We can't make a move without the Security Police closing in.'

'When are you due there?' Spencer asked.

'The day after tomorrow,' Maxwell replied, 'but I can bring it forward. I could fly in to-morrow.'

'You do,' Spencer said.

'What about you?'

'I have to return to Athens,' Spencer said, 'but I'll notify our Cairo office.' He paused and looked at Fletcher. 'There is one other person who might be able to help us,' he said.

'Ali?' Fletcher asked.

'That's him,' Spencer said.

'I was wondering about Ali,' Fletcher said thoughtfully, 'but he hasn't been able to supply anything of merit for a long time.'

'But he keeps himself well informed,' Spencer growled. 'You say the man who knifed Timovsky looked like an Arab. If the Russians are recruiting the scum from the bazaars to do their dirty work Ali might know about it. He might even be able to help you with Breznov. He's always interested in a proposition.'

In a country where every beggar was a potential cutthroat, murderer, procurer, or smuggler, the man Spencer was referring to was a king. If money could buy it, Ali could get it. But whether his contacts reached into the corners of the Foreign Office was something of which Fletcher was sceptical. But he agreed it was worth a try. They were going to have to pull out all the stops.

'What about this K business?' Maxwell asked.

'Means nothing to me,' Spencer confessed.

'Nor me,' Fletcher added.

Maxwell gave a long, deep sigh.

'How will we keep in touch?' he said.

'Normal channels,' Spencer said. 'Through the Embassies.'

They sat playing with their glasses, but nothing more was said. It all depended on Cairo.

Maxwell was the first to leave. He polished off his drink and slipped quietly into the deserted lane of the bazaar.

After he had gone, Spencer recharged Fletcher's glass.

'Good man, Maxwell,' he said, 'but they don't like setbacks. Take badly to it.'

So he had sensed the anxiety as well, Fletcher thought.

'They have good reason,' Fletcher said. 'They've suffered more than us.'

'We've been here longer,' Spencer said irritably. 'We should be able to protect our agents better.'

'What about Timovsky?' Fletcher asked pointedly.

Spencer looked up at him and saw the hard look on his face.

'What about him?' he growled.

'Where was his protection?'

'We can't fight their internal security machine, damn it,' Spencer snapped and turned his attention back to his glass.

'So you think their internal security caught up with him?' Fletcher asked evenly.

'Yes I do,' Spencer retorted. 'Timovsky was sent home because he was suspect. He had only a limited life for us. We knew that.'

'I'm surprised he ever came back,' Fletcher said.

'Probably to use him.'

'I hope you are right,' Fletcher said meaningly. 'Otherwise...'

'Don't start a witch hunt,' Spencer warned. 'It can prove dangerous. We have work to do.' He placed his handkerchief in his pocket. It was an indication that their meeting was drawing to a close.

Fletcher shrugged. He didn't share Spencer's optimism. The dead Russian worried him, and it would keep on worrying him until he found out how the K.G.B. caught up with their man.

'You can't stay in Istanbul,' Spencer said. 'They'll make a lot of noise, even if it is with empty cans.'

'What did you have in mind?' Fletcher asked.

'Cairo,' Spencer said casually. 'And Ali.'

Good, Fletcher thought. He wasn't in the mood for a monastic rest until the hue and cry died down. He wanted action. Cairo could give him that and more.

'What about Hamilton?' he asked. 'Do I work with him?'

Hamilton was Spencer's man on the ground in Cairo.

'No,' Spencer said. 'I have plans for Hamilton. He will have his hands full. You take care of Ali. If it leads anywhere you can always contact Hamilton.'

'Any limit?' Fletcher asked.

Spencer mentally wrestled with the problem. He was torn between his natural desire to curb expenditure and wanting to get the information. Ali could be expensive, that was why they didn't make more use of him. He finally gave judgement in favour of the cause.

'We'll pay anything within reason,' he grumbled. 'Ali has an account with a Swiss Bank. We'll pay direct on verification of the information.'

There was nothing else to be said. It all depended now upon what the next few days would bring from Cairo.

The ball had bounced to yet another corner.

Chapter Two

Two days later Fletcher arrived in Port Said. In a crowded, sun-drenched, customs shed, he lost himself amongst the cosmopolitan gathering of passengers who had disembarked from a Greek passenger ship. A ship Fletcher had joined the previous day in Beirut, as a third class passenger. He travelled on a Greek passport, as an agent for a Greek trading company. His appearance, in a soiled, white linen suit, and carrying a green canvas suitcase, resembled many of the other third class passengers who bustled and harassed the officials.

This was not Fletcher's normal method of entry into the country, nor the safest, but it was more expedient than the back door route, and attracted less attention than the more sophisticated air flight.

He passed through the customs without any difficulty and quickly rid himself of his newly made acquaintances.

It was late in the afternoon when he arrived in Cairo. The city was hot, congested, noisy and oppressive. He mingled with the dark faces which filled the pavements until he felt satisfied that he was not being followed, and then took a bus into one of the modern suburbs of the city. He registered at a respectable, quiet hotel, in a secluded avenue overlooking the Nile, and waited patiently for nightfall.

As soon as it turned dark he slipped out of the hotel, and went in search of the man he hoped would help him – Ali. This was not the Egyptian's true name, but it was the one used by British Intelligence. Ali was a man with a background as complex as his real name, a mixture of Syrian and Egyptian. He was not a regular informer. He was more concerned with the less delicate issues of smuggling and gun-running, but as Spencer had indicated, he was a man of many connections and a love of money. He operated with only a limited amount of caution from a night club called the El-Giza, on the fringe of the bazaars. A club which was popular with tourists because it gave them what they expected in Cairo – the decor of old Egypt and a bevy of belly dancers.

When Fletcher arrived at the club it had already acquired a modest group of tourists who sat in the scented cabaret room, eating kebabs and kafta. He made his request to see Ali to one of the many white coated attendants who kept a watchful eye on the affairs of the club, and was ushered into the cocktail bar whilst his message was relayed to Ali's office. Like the cabaret room, the bar had its quota of visitors. Fletcher ordered a drink and sat in one of the darkened corners, and surveyed the occupants of the room. His eyes fell upon a girl in her early twenties, sitting at one of the tables, and he was immediately struck by her beauty. She had long, dark brown hair, and the type of face which could have graced the cover of any magazine – dark eyes, high cheek bones, and a full mouth. She was wearing a plain white dress which accentuated her golden brown tan. She was not alone, but she could have been for all the attention she was giving her companion – a dark, sullen faced man, who sat staring into the room. Fletcher toyed with his glass, mildly curious as to their relationship. He saw the girl look up sharply, and followed her eyes to the curtained opening which led to Ali's office, where a smartly dressed, middle aged man had suddenly appeared. He was a tall, erect man, with a long, thin face, and deep set, unfriendly eyes. Fletcher watched him look around the room until he caught sight of the girl, when he smiled and crossed over to her table. The girl stood up to greet him. For a few seconds they held a conversation and then the man led the girl out of the room. The girl's other escort followed dutifully behind like a servant. Fletcher watched them leave and wondered what their business with Ali had been about.

Soon after, the bar attendant gave him the

all clear. He finished his drink and slipped through the curtained opening and entered Ali's office.

Ali stood up from behind his desk to greet him. He was not a big man, and in appearance looked like many other Egyptians – dark, with sleek black hair and a sharp face. He was immaculately dressed, however, in an expensive dinner suit.

'Come and sit down,' he said in a business-like tone, not unfriendly, but at the same time not patronizing.

Fletcher sat facing the Egyptian.

'What can I do for you?' Ali asked, forgoing the customary pleasantries and platitudes.

'Information,' Fletcher said.

Ali shrugged, non-committally.

'About what?' he asked.

'It is whispered that the Russians have re-cruited the Arab fellahin to do their dirty work, so that the Russians will not get their hands fouled.'

'The Russians are not the only ones who take advantage of the surplus labour market here in Cairo,' Ali replied.

'True,' Fletcher agreed, 'but it is also said that the Russians are using them abroad. Istanbul for instance. Two days ago.'

'I have not heard of this,' Ali said seriously.

'They are not broadcasting it,' Fletcher pointed out.

Ali pushed a silver cigarette box across the

table. Fletcher politely refused.

'How can I help you?' Ali asked, lighting a cigarette and allowing the smoke to come out of his nostrils.

'You can ask your many friends if they know anything about this. I am very interested.'

Ali didn't appear enthusiastic. 'I will ask,' he said. 'Perhaps we may hear of something. I do not know.'

He wasn't being so helpful as he had been in the past, Fletcher thought. His other interests must be proving more profitable. There was also the question of Breznov's visit. Fletcher didn't hold out much hope, but he decided to try.

'A Russian called Breznov is visiting Cairo,' Fletcher said quietly, 'I would like to know who he is seeing and what is being discussed.'

Ali raised his eyebrows.

'A tall order,' he muttered.

'In which case it will be well rewarded,' Fletcher added.

But Ali didn't bite.

'Times have changed since you were last here, my friend,' he said in a sad tone. 'We have had a war which we lost.' He threw up his hands. 'The Security Police are everywhere. One false move and...' He ran his fingers across his throat and again threw up his arms in despair.

'But you manage to remain in business,'

35

Fletcher pointed out.

'Ah yes, but the profits are less. I have heavy expenses now, and besides, it is not a matter of state security.'

So they accept smuggling, gun running, and dope peddling, so long as they get their cut, Fletcher thought, but not espionage. They had their own code of honour.

'It would pay very well,' Fletcher persisted, knowing Ali's weakness.

'How well?' Ali asked, but added, 'I am only curious.'

'Name your price,' Fletcher said.

This time Ali did look impressed. He leant back in his chair and sat solemnly studying Fletcher as if trying to read his mind.

'You want this information that badly?' he asked.

Fletcher grunted, but didn't commit himself. He knew Ali was taking the bait.

Ali suddenly gave a half laugh of despair. 'It is impossible,' he said. 'Impossible.'

Fletcher didn't give up. 'I'll leave it with you,' he said, 'and call back.'

'Yes, yes,' Ali said eagerly. 'Come back tomorrow evening. Who can tell?'

Fletcher didn't waste any further time. He knew Ali was interested. If he could get hold of anything he would be in the market. If he couldn't, Fletcher would have to try elsewhere.

He returned to the now crowded cocktail

36

bar, took in the brown and pink faces and decided to leave them to it. As he entered the foyer, a burst of applause came from the cabaret room and its darkened atmosphere suddenly became an orange glow. Fletcher hesitated, glanced into the room, and saw the groups of tourists squatting around short-legged tables under a haze of cigarette smoke. He was attracted to a nearby group by the sound of their American accents. They were a party of five, four men and a woman, and he noticed the dark, laughing face of the woman, held the full attention of her companions. Sitting next to her was a tall, lean, young looking man, who was finding his sitting position not suitable to his build. Next to him was another man, a more elderly man – a man Fletcher immediately recognized. It was Maxwell. He was also giving the woman his full attention. Fletcher turned his attention to the two other men in the party, but as the room drifted again into darkness, he saw Maxwell look up in his direction. Fletcher gave no sign of recognition and turned and left the foyer.

From the brightly lit entrance to the club he quickly walked over to where the cars were parked, and kept himself hidden in the shadows. A few minutes later he saw Maxwell leave the club and cross over to the park. Fletcher joined him.

'If I'd known he was on your shopping list,

I would have kept clear,' Maxwell smiled.

'Sight-seeing?' Fletcher asked.

'A party of official Embassy visitors,' Maxwell explained. 'Seemed a good opportunity to make a few calls.'

'Who is the woman?'

'Dr Marsh,' Maxwell said. 'One of the party. How did you make out?'

'He is not very enthusiastic,' Fletcher said ruefully. 'I'll know better tomorrow evening.'

'Pity,' Maxwell muttered. 'I'll give him a miss and leave him to you.'

'Any other news about our friend?'

'No, damn it, except that the Iraqui Defence Minister is also in Cairo. It could be significant.'

A car drove into the park illuminating the area with its bright headlamps.

'I'd better be getting back,' Maxwell said. 'I'll see you in Athens. I am leaving the day after tomorrow.'

Fletcher stepped back into the shadows and watched Maxwell walk back to the club. As Maxwell approached the entrance, Fletcher saw another figure appear, as if out of the darkness, and join Maxwell under the projecting canopy. It was the tall man who had been sitting next to Maxwell at the table. Fletcher watched them disappear inside the club and wondered why the other man had also left the party.

From the native quarter of the city, Fletcher returned to the vicinity of his hotel by foot and public transport. He alighted from a bus, passed a lone car parked on the otherwise deserted boulevard, and entered the narrow lane which led to his hotel. It was a poorly lit street and he had only gone a few yards when he sensed a feeling of danger. It was an intuition which he had developed in the same way as an engineer senses a fault with the mechanics of his engine. It distinguished the professionals from the amateurs. Something was amiss.

He walked warily along the pavement.

Suddenly someone was upon him! With a yell and a leap a figure jumped at him from the dark shadows. Fletcher swung around with the fury of a lion and met his assailant in mid-air. He was fighting for his life – this was no wayside assault. He caught a flash of steel in his attacker's hand and desperately held the arm away from his body. The assailant grunted and forced the knife towards Fletcher's chest. Fletcher held it back and then suddenly gave way. As the figure lunged forward, Fletcher fell backwards, twisted his body, and pulled the figure with him. The two bodies fell heavily onto the hard surface, but Fletcher was on top and there was no time to lose his advantage. Swiftly he brought his knee up to his attacker's chin, crashing his head onto the pavement. The body beneath him momentarily sagged. Fletcher knocked the knife out of the man's hand and got hold of it before the man regained his breath.

With eyes ablaze Fletcher dragged the body into an upright position and pinned it against the wall of a nearby building. His attacker didn't look like an Arab fellah, but his long, dark face, still had all the Arabic trademarks. He was one of the modern, white suited middle class, Fletcher thought. One of the more intelligent cutthroats. The man's eyes still looked dull and glazed from the blow to his head.

Fletcher gripped the man's jacket by the lapels and brought the point of the knife into contact with the man's throat.

'Who sent you?' Fletcher hissed in Arabic.

The man didn't reply and Fletcher added pressure to the knife.

'Who sent you?' he hissed again. He meant business.

The Arab saw the look in Fletcher's eyes and opened his mouth. Fletcher increased the pressure fractionally, and the Arab cried out. It was a plea for mercy, but it was in a tongue which Fletcher didn't recognize! Puzzled, Fletcher eased the pressure of the knife, and again the Arab uttered a strange cry. At the same instance something smacked into the wall above their heads spraying them with dust. It was followed by the whine of a bullet which also smacked into the wall.

Someone was firing at them with a revolver fitted with a silencer! And they weren't particular who they hit! Fletcher dived into the nearby shadows and scurried away on all fours. The Arab ran for his life.

Fletcher lay still and waited. The shooting had stopped. He turned and looked along the lane to the illuminated boulevard and saw a saloon car drive past. There were two figures in it. His two would-be assassins! He picked himself up and brushed his clothing. Who had sent them? he wondered. Was this Ali's doing? Or had he been spotted in Port Said by one of the Soviet's many agents, who kept a close watch on all comings and goings? In a country where labour was cheap, they had an army. Somebody knew he was in Cairo and didn't welcome his presence. He was going to have to watch his step. The man with the gun appeared to have as little regard for his friend's life as he did for Fletcher's.

Thoughtfully he returned to his hotel. The man who had attacked him had looked like an Egyptian Arab, but his cry had been in a tongue which Fletcher didn't recognize. Yet there had been something familiar about it. He had heard it before. Where? He racked his brains, but it didn't register. Mentally he stored it in the back of his mind. It would come to him.

At the hotel he paid his account in advance, collected his gear, and slipped out of the building by a rear entrance. Whoever was interested in him knew his whereabouts. It was time to move on.

He booked into another hotel in a busier part of the city where the bright lights and constant movement of people gave a measure of protection. They would find him again, but it would take time and he wasn't planning to stay much longer.

In his bedroom he locked the balcony doors and lay on the bed smoking a cigarette. The knife the attacker had used was not unlike the one that had killed Timovsky. Was that significant? he wondered. And the Russian's murderer had looked like an Arab. Was there any connection?

He turned his attention to an evening newspaper he had picked up en route. He didn't expect to see Breznov's movements reported, but he was curious to see if any reference was made to the arrival of the Iraqui Defence Minister.

The main headlines were concerned with a series of anti-west demonstrations which had broken out in Baghdad, and the remaining articles on the front sheet were propaganda items cajoling the people to greater efforts of national unity. Fletcher turned to the inside page and was immediately attracted to a photograph showing the arrival at Cairo Airport of a visiting party of officials of the American Peace Corps. The picture showed four men and a woman, and it was the woman who held his attention. She was the same person he had previously seen that evening at the El Giza Club with Maxwell. And so were two of the men. Fletcher read the article carefully. The party was led by a Dr Paul Bradshaw, an assistant director of the Peace Corps for the Middle East. The other members of the party were given as Carl Lipman, Vincent Marlow, and Dr Carol Marsh. They were visiting Cairo for two days as part of a tour of inspection which had taken in Tehran, Baghdad and Damascus. After Cairo they were to visit Athens before returning to their headquarters in Turkey. They were staying at the Carlton Hotel and during their visit they were to have talks with the Egyptian Minister of the Interior. They were also giving a lecture the following morning at Cairo University to explain the nature of the work of the Peace Corps.

Fletcher got off the bed and started to pace the floor. There had also been a report of the movements of this particular party of Americans on the newspaper cutting he had found on the Russian. Had that been accidental or intentional? They had all been very quick to attribute the cutting as a reference to the firms the Soviet trade delegation were keen to do business with, but was that really the case? Had Timovsky not been more concerned with the tour of inspection being made by the American Party? A tour which took them to a number of capitals, and brought them into contact with many high Government officials!

Fletcher wondered... The cutting found on the Russian had been taken from a newspaper and this was the only report which had not been torn. Even one of the firms underlined on the reverse side had been torn through its name. Surely Timovsky would have been more careful. He picked up the newspaper again and re-read the article. It was strange, he thought, that they should be in Cairo at the same time that Breznov was visiting the city. Very strange.

He scanned through the remainder of the newspaper, but as he had come to expect, there was no reference to the visit of the Iraqui Defence Minister. But now Fletcher had two items to nag at the back of his mind. First there was the Arab who had attacked him. His short outburst when Fletcher had added the extra pressure to the knife at his throat, had not been in Arabic. Fletcher wanted to know what language he had spoken. Now there was also the question of the visiting members of the American Peace Corps. Did it have any significance, or was it purely coincidental? He made a quick decision. He couldn't satisfy his curiosity over the first problem, but he could with the second. If the Americans were giving a lecture the following morning, then there was no reason why he shouldn't attend it. At least he would learn something about the nature of their work, and if it was completely innocent no harm would come of it. If their visit had other implications, the sooner he stirred it up the better. A little easier in his mind he retired for the night.

At ten-thirty, precisely, the following morning, Fletcher left his hotel and at eleven o'clock was intermingling with the students at the University as they crowded into the assembly hall. It wasn't difficult for Fletcher to become one of the masses. All that he required was a pair of slacks and an open-fronted white shirt. His sun-tanned face and dark hair was only a shade paler than the other faces in the hall.

It was a large hall with a tiled floor and a series of ceiling fans which hummed as they swirled the hot air around the room. Along both sides of the hall were arched openings, and Fletcher purposely selected a seat close to one of them. The students who sat around him talked noisily to each other, and left him to his own thoughts.

After a short wait the official party mounted the platform and the noise subsided. There were three Americans on the platform and two University officials, but at the entrance to the hall Fletcher noticed two heavily-built Egyptians who both looked every inch a policeman. Standing close to them Fletcher recognized the tall, fresh-faced American he had seen the previous evening in the club, but who had not been on the photograph in the newspaper.

The American party on the platform consisted of Dr Bradshaw, Dr Carol Marsh and Carl Lipman. As one of the University officials made his speech of welcome, Fletcher studied the three Americans. Dr Bradshaw was a tall, well-made man, in his sixties, with rather stern features and silver-grey hair. Carol Marsh was a woman whose age was difficult to place, but Fletcher put her in her late thirties. She wore a pair of rimless spectacles which made her features look less attractive than he had noticed the previous evening. She had a round, dark face, and jet-black hair. Her figure was trim and well proportioned, and could have been displayed to better advantage than was permitted by her plain cotton dress.

As Fletcher turned his attention to the third number of their party, the Egyptian finished his opening address of welcome, and Dr Bradshaw took the rostrum.

'In his inaugural address the late President Kennedy said, ask not what your country can do for you, ask what can you do for your country. That ladies and gentlemen is one of the expressions of ideas behind our Peace Corps.'

Dr Bradshaw's voice rang out loud and clear and he paused to allow the University official to repeat his statement in Arabic. Fletcher looked at Carl Lipman. He was a studious-looking man in his earlier forties, of medium height and build. He sat cross-legged on his seat, with a bent head and a serious expression on his face.

'We want to fight problems, not people, is another expression of our ideas.'

Again the Doctor paused to allow the translator to repeat his statement.

'And so on March 1st, 1961, an executive order established the Corps on a temporary basis.'

The Doctor and his translator continued to give the historical background and the development of the Peace Corps up to its present position. Their volunteers helped as teachers, community workers, agricultural and engineering workers, and as medical and public administration assistants. As the Doctor expanded upon the nature of their work and the results of their labours, it became abundantly clear that many countries were indebted to them. Their tentacles reached out into the outlying under-developed provinces, and provided a social service unequalled anywhere else in the world.

Fletcher listened to the address and admired both the Doctor's masterly, forthright manner, and also the deeds and intentions of his workers. But when the Doctor explained the nature of the tour carried out by his party, Fletcher wondered whether it was also being put to the benefit of other causes. From Ankara the party had visited Eastern Turkey, Persia, Iraq, and Jordan. After Egypt they were visiting Greece before returning to Turkey. Their journey had taken them through a number of countries where Western Intelligence had suffered a number of suspicious setbacks. It was a coincidence that Fletcher felt deserved attention, especially in view of the newspaper cutting found on the dying Russian.

When the American had finished his address, he threw the meeting open to questions. Hesitantly one or two students stood up and questioned him about certain aspects of the Corps work. The Doctor answered the questions confidently. But when a student, a few rows behind Fletcher, stood up and asked if the Americans were not using the platform as a means of Western propaganda, the atmosphere in the hall suddenly changed. From across the hall came a cry of derision. The student, however, was not to be put off. He appealed to the assembly not to be taken in by the propaganda. Fletcher turned in his seat to see who was asking the questions and found that it was not a student, but a heavily-built, dark-skinned, professional-looking agitator! As Fletcher turned his eyes away from him they fell straight on the person sitting alongside the man. It was the same face that he had looked into the previous evening in the alleyway! And next to him was another face he recognized! It was the man who had been sitting with the girl in the cocktail bar at Ali's club! Quickly he turned his back on them. If he was seen in the room he might never get out alive!

Anxiously he listened to the heated exchange of words which started to flow back and forward across the assembly hall. The Americans became a back number as the two rival factions yelled abuse at each other. Then it happened. A movement of a chair, innocent or otherwise, was followed by the levitation of another chair from one side of the hall to the other. A scuffle immediately followed, and all around Fletcher students were standing up and moving into the centre of the hall, where the affray appeared to be at its height. Fletcher saw the American party leave the platform and decided it was time for him to leave also. But it was no easy task. He was surrounded by students clammering to get into the battle. Furiously, he lashed out with his fists and cleared a way to the arched opening. It was as he reached his goal that he caught sight of the girl he had seen in Ali's club. She was several rows ahead of him, nearer the platform, and like Fletcher she was also trying to get clear of the bustling students. The frightened expression on her face as she realized she was not going to reach the exit, made Fletcher turn back. Again he lashed out with his fists and legs until he could grab her arm and pull her clear. As he pushed her out of the building he heard the shrill sound of a police whistle, but he didn't wait to see if it had any effect. Still gripping the girl's arm, he pulled her across the grassed quadrangle and through an opening between two buildings. When they came to the road which ran past the Students' Union, he stopped running. The girl's hair hung loosely over her face, and her head was bent as she panted for breath. Fletcher saw a nearby bench seat and half carried her to it. Gradually she regained her composure. She brushed her hair back from her face and managed a faint smile.

'Myya,' she said pleadingly. 'Myya minfadolk.'

She wanted water.

Fletcher glanced up at the Students' Union building. There would be a water fountain inside. He ran up the steps and soon found the fountain. He filled a paper carton and hurried back to the girl. But the seat was empty – the girl had gone!

Thoughtfully he drank the water himself. There was no doubt in his mind now about which intelligence agency had tried to have him killed the previous evening, and had paid the same men to break up the meeting. They were working for the Russians. But where did the girl fit into the picture? She had not been sitting with the man Fletcher had seen her with in Ali's club, and if it hadn't been for Fletcher's assistance she would have been at the mercy of an unruly mob of students. Just what was her association with them? And the man who had been doing business with Ali? Was he also one of them? Was he also working for the Russians? Fletcher didn't like it. Ali was a businessman with a love of money and little respect for politics or allegiances. Was he now also working for the opposition?

The noise from the Assembly Hall became even more belligerent. Fletcher decided to follow the girl's example and get clear of the area before serious trouble developed.

For the remainder of the afternoon he kept himself out of harm's way in a shaded part of the Garden City on the banks of the Nile. He was more puzzled than ever about the American party. He had no grounds for real suspicion, but the presence at the meeting of the Arab who had tried to kill him was another coincidence which left an unpleasant taste.

When Fletcher returned to the club that evening, he made his entrance by the side door to the kitchen, as a safeguard against any unwelcome observers. He announced

51

himself to the large, armed Sudanese, who was there for the very purpose of preventing such entrances, and was eventually allowed to proceed to Ali's office.

Ali was pouring out two drinks from a bottle of Scotch when Fletcher joined him. Fletcher recognized the gesture. They were going to do business.

Fletcher accepted the drink and exchanged the customary pleasantries, prepared to let Ali make the play.

'I have made many enquiries about the matter we discussed last night,' Ali said as he poured the second drink.

'And?'

Ali shrugged. 'If it is as you say, then my friends know nothing about it.'

Fletcher felt disappointed. The man who had killed Timovsky had Arabic features, there was no mistaking that, but it had been a long shot in thinking that Ali could have found anything out about him. The Arab world covered a large area and included many people.

'However, I might be able to help you with the other matter,' Ali said brightly.

Fletcher was taken aback, but didn't show it. Espionage was not normally in Ali's line.

'At a price of course,' Ali added.

'Of course,' Fletcher agreed, with a faint trace of sarcasm in his voice which passed over the Egyptian's head.

'I have made contact with a man who works in the Foreign Office. He has run into certain financial difficulties, I am told, and could be persuaded to take up photography, as a paying hobby.'

'How much?' Fletcher asked.

'One hundred pounds,' Ali smiled and hurriedly added: 'That is his price, of course. I also have mine.'

'Which is?'

'Another two for me,' Ali said quickly.

'Expensive,' Fletcher muttered.

'But worth it,' Ali beamed.

'A lot depends on what success your friend has with his new hobby,' Fletcher said not committing himself.

'Breznov is leaving Cairo tomorrow to return to Moscow,' Ali said quietly. 'Today he has had a meeting with the Foreign Secretary and the Iraqui Defence Minister.'

Ali's statement sounded authentic, Fletcher thought, in view of what Maxwell had told him.

'A report has been prepared,' Ali continued, 'giving an account of the decisions made at the meeting. It is being sent to the President.' Ali leant forward and delivered his trump card. 'I might be able to get you a copy of that report,' he said proudly.

Fletcher's face remained impassive, but he was impressed. It was because of Breznov that he had come to Cairo – Breznov and the dying Timovsky. If Ali could deliver a photostat of the Russians' meeting with the two Arab Ministers, Fletcher's work was finished.

'Interested?' Ali asked.

Very, Fletcher thought, but it all sounded too easy. It troubled him. He leant on the table and gave Ali a long, hard look.

'I'm interested,' he said, 'if you are on the level.'

Ali's face paled. 'Why should I not be on the level?' he asked incredulously.

'Because someone tried to kill me last night,' Fletcher said pointedly.

'I know nothing of this, I assure you,' Ali pleaded.

'One of the men who attacked me had a friend in your club last night.'

'Come,' Ali said with forced lightness, 'There are many people who visit my club.'

'This man was with a girl, sitting in your bar. A very attractive girl. They were waiting for a man who was with you. A tall, thin-faced man.'

Ali looked serious.

'I have many business interests,' he said barely above a whisper, 'and many connections. People come and go, but what they do outside the club is their own business, not mine. I assure you I know nothing, absolutely nothing, of this attack which was made upon you.'

Fletcher sat back and studied Ali's deadpan expression. Ali was a past master at lying, but on this occasion Fletcher was prepared to give him the benefit of the doubt. He had no alternative. He wanted a copy of the report. Nevertheless, he decided to put Ali's loyalty to the test.

'All right,' Fletcher said cheerfully. 'We have a deal, on one condition?'

'Condition?' Ali asked. 'Are you in a position to make conditions?'

Fletcher shrugged.

'Perhaps not,' he smiled, 'but let us make a gesture to show that we have a mutual confidence. All I want is a little information about your business contact.'

'And what do I get?'

'Another fifty?' Fletcher asked.

'So be it,' Ali said, but without enthusiasm. 'Who was the man you spoke with, and the girl?'

Ali hesitated before replying. 'The man is Mustafa Kaddir,' he said finally. 'The girl is called Reba. She is his niece.'

Kaddir! Fletcher's pulse quickened as he mentally repeated the name, Kaddir! It was an unusual name yet it closely resembled the name Timovsky had been uttering in his dying breaths. Kaddir! And he was here in Cairo at the same time as Breznov. Another unusual coincidence.

'What did he want?' Fletcher asked.

'He approached me three days ago and asked if I could arrange a purchase of arms for him. I have made the necessary overtures on his behalf. It is out of my hands now. An international syndicate have taken over. He will be contacted by them.'

'Here in Cairo?'

'No,' Ali sighed. 'Since the Security Police have started to run our country my friends on the Continent have decided to move headquarters to a less vulnerable location. In fact they have moved to your part of the world – Pireaus!'

This wasn't news to Fletcher. In the past year the crowded seaport of Athens had become the nerve centre for the international smuggling and dope-running syndicates. It had become the gateway between the underworlds of the Continent and the Middle East.

'Where is he from?' Fletcher asked.

Ali threw up his arms despairingly.

'Please,' he said, 'no more questions. I assure you he is not from your province. He is from the East.'

'Where,' Fletcher insisted. He had to know.

Ali made a resigned gesture.

'Kandahar province,' he muttered. 'He is a local chieftain.'

Afghanistan, Fletcher thought. It was out of his area, but still within the orbit of British Intelligence. They were concerned with

56

anyone who was receiving arms, no matter where, and Afghanistan wasn't far away. He wondered if Ali was telling the truth. Kaddir's mannerisms had had all the sophisticated trademarks of a strong western influence. He was something more than the local tribal chieftain that Ali suggested. But what? Fletcher thought of the man who had attacked him. Had his plea for mercy been in Afghan? He thought not, but he couldn't be certain.

'You believe that?' Fletcher asked.

Ali shrugged. 'That is what he tells me – I do not question him. I cannot afford to.'

'Yes, you can,' Fletcher said lightly. 'I will pay you.' He wanted to know more about Kaddir, a lot more.

Ali's face relaxed as it always did when money was mentioned. 'It might take time,' he said, 'I cannot afford to upset my friends on the Continent.'

He was referring to his connection with the all-powerful smuggling syndicate. They could get rough. He was prepared to sell the information when Kaddir had been passed over. Well, Fletcher thought, he could wait, and if Kaddir was going to Piraeus, Ali might not be necessary. Fletcher had many contacts in Piraeus and Athens. It was his base.

'Where will he be in Piraeus?' he asked.

But this time Ali was firm.

'I do not know anything,' he said. 'All I know is that he will be contacted there. Nothing else.'

'O.K., then, we'll leave it at that,' Fletcher said and turned his thoughts back to getting a copy of the report.

'When do I collect the report?' he asked.

'If all goes well, I will have a copy by tomorrow evening. If all does not go well...' He left the rest unsaid.

'Here?' Fletcher asked.

Ali looked thoughtful.

'No,' he said. 'Come to my villa, it will be safer. Do you know Al Gida Street?'

Fletcher said he would find it.

'There is a side street leading down to the river, Mazira Street. My villa is number seven. Come at nine p.m. As for the money – get your Government to pay it into my bank at Zurich.'

Fletcher made a mental note of the arrangements.

'Take care of yourself,' he said. 'I wouldn't like anything to happen to you before tomorrow night.'

'It won't,' Ali assured him, confidently.

Fletcher left soon afterwards, again via the kitchens. He returned to his hotel, locked himself in his room, and made his plans for the following day. If Ali produced the promised report, he had to get it to Spencer for translation as soon as possible. He had to

hand it over to Hamilton imm
brought out a street map o
located Ali's villa. Close by v
logical Gardens. It was an ideal
to meet Hamilton. He laid a sq
over the street map and moved
he found a suitable location to use as a base
for his co-ordinates. Mentally he worked out
the map reference and translated it into a
simple code.

Having satisfied himself that he had his
message for passing to Hamilton, he then
checked the sailing times from Port Said to
Piraeus. But there wasn't a sailing scheduled
until the morning following his meeting
with Ali, and he didn't want to stay in Cairo,
or Egypt, longer than necessary. He checked
the airflights and found that the U.A.A. had
a plane leaving for Athens at midnight. He
decided to take this flight and risk being
observed at the airport.

Before turning in, he checked the locks on
the bedroom and balcony doors and placed
his automatic under his pillow. The next
twenty-four hours were going to be critical.

Early the following morning Fletcher left
his hotel. He went to the railway station,
deposited his case in the left luggage office,
and in a public telephone kiosk dialled Hamilton's private number. When Hamilton answered his call, he quickly passed his coded
message.

the railway station, he went to the
s of the U.A.A. in Opera Square, and
oked a seat on the flight to Athens leaving
Cairo airport that evening.

For the remainder of the day he made
himself as discreet as possible and kept a
close watch on the dark faces which came
close to him. It was with a feeling of relief
that he eventually made his way to Ali's villa
a few minutes before the scheduled time of
nine p.m.

The villa was a white cubed building surrounded by palm trees and a high stone
wall. It was in a quiet, dimly-lit street, and
only the presence of a number of large
American cars confirmed that the people
lived behind the shuttered windows.

Ali's villa also looked deserted, but in response to his knock Ali himself opened the
heavy, iron-studded, entrance door. He
stood in the entrance hall wearing his usual
garb of evening dress. Fletcher noticed his
face looked tense. He beckoned Fletcher to
enter, and took him into an adjoining room
exquisitely furnished with expensive drapes
and thick Persian rugs. Ali went straight to a
cocktail cabinet and produced a bottle. He
offered Fletcher a drink, but Fletcher refused and came straight the point.

'I can only presume that you have got the
goods,' he said.

Ali sank his drink.

'Yes,' he said. 'I have.'

'You have done well,' Fletcher said. 'It will pay you to keep your contact interested in photography. I have a friend in Cairo who will be very pleased.' He was thinking of Hamilton.

Ali declined the invitation, rather too quickly Fletcher thought.

'This is not in my normal line of business,' he said. 'It is too dangerous. The Security Police are everywhere.'

In which case it made their present transaction all the more suspicious, Fletcher thought.

Ali turned to a bureau, unlocked a drawer, and withdrew a small roll of micro-film. He handed it to Fletcher.

'It is all there,' he said. 'You can examine it if you wish.'

Fletcher unrolled the film, laid it flat under a table lamp, and examined it through a magnifying glass. The letters were too small for him to read clearly, but it appeared to be what Ali claimed.

'I assure you, it is a copy of the report sent to the President,' Ali said.

Fletcher pocketed the film.

'You won't forget our other business,' he said and added, 'shall we say another hundred?'

Ali looked at him from behind his glass.

'It is early days,' he said very quietly and

61

turned his eyes on a desk calendar. Fletcher watched him flick over the plastic date cards until it showed a date four days ahead. That was when Ali would have the information. But by that time the deal would be finalised, Fletcher thought, and Kaddir would have vanished. He was going to have to look for Kaddir himself. However, Ali might still be of use.

'You will be contacted,' he said.

'It has been a pleasure doing business with you,' Ali smiled, and led Fletcher out of the room.

In the hallway the two men parted company. Fletcher slipped out into the darkness again and Ali returned to his cocktail cabinet. As he poured himself another drink, a side door opened and a figure entered the room.

'Satisfactory?' Ali asked.

'Very,' came the reply. 'Except that you talk too much.'

Ali opened his mouth to protest, but no words came out. Two muffled shots from a revolver silenced him for good.

Chapter Three

When Fletcher reached the entrance to the Zoological Gardens, a black saloon car drew up alongside him. Quickly the micro-film changed hands and the car drove swiftly away. Fletcher also cleared the area and made his way to the railway terminal. He collected his case from the luggage office and left the station via a rear exit. In Helwar Street he picked up a taxi and arrived at the airport with a few minutes to spare. He checked in at the flight desk, and sat on a settee where he could see everyone who entered the building. A short while later his flight was announced, and he passed into the departure bay glad to be leaving Cairo and Ali to Hamilton.

As he took his seat on the plane, two last minute arrivals joined the flight. One was Dr Bradshaw, the man who had given the lecture at the University. With him was a man Fletcher recognized as an official from the American Embassy in Athens. He had a worried expression on his face, as if the relief of having made the flight deadline had not caught up with him. As they took their seats, Fletcher glanced around at the faces of the other passengers, and saw that no other member of the American party were aboard. He made himself comfortable and thought about Ali and Kaddir, but Dr Bradshaw's presence triggered off his suspicions about the Americans. Again he wondered whether the reference to their visit to Tehran, on the newspaper cutting found on Timovsky, had any hidden meaning? It was a question which wouldn't leave him alone.

The American party was not his only worry. There was also the two Arabs who had tried to kill him. What was there about the Arab's cry that had sounded familiar? Where had they come from?

When Fletcher arrived at Athens Airport he was no nearer solving any of his problems.

Dr Bradshaw and his companion were given V.I.P. treatment and whisked away in an Embassy car. Fletcher watched thoughtfully from a distance and decided he would feel happier if he kept close to the American party. He made a brief, cryptic telephone call to Spencer to let him know that he had returned, and left the terminal building and walked quickly along the row of waiting taxis until he found the one he wanted. It was operated by a small, jovial-faced Greek, called Toni, who was one of Fletcher's many contacts in the Greek capital. The Greek was dozing in the front seat of his cab, but quickly awoke when Fletcher spoke to him. The two men greeted each other warmly, then Fletcher got down to business.

'Have a party of Americans arrived from Cairo today?' he asked. 'Probably three men and a woman. They are Embassy officials.'

Toni shrugged apologetically. 'I do not know,' he said, 'but I will ask.'

'Find out where they are staying,' Fletcher said and added, 'There is also another party I am interested in.' He gave Toni a description of Kaddir and his niece.

The Greek left his cab, but returned a few minutes later.

'A party of Americans arrived on a flight from Cairo at four o'clock this afternoon,' he said. 'There were four men and one woman. They were met by two men from the American Embassy.'

'Good,' Fletcher said eagerly. 'Where are they staying?'

'At the Grand Hotel.'

The largest and most expensive hotel in Piraeus, Fletcher thought. It figured.

'And the other party?' he asked hopefully.

Toni shook his head. 'Nothing,' he muttered.

Fletcher hadn't expected there would be. If he knew Kaddir, he would be more discreet. But he had to be found. Fletcher glanced at his watch. It was not the time for making plans.

'Let's go,' he said.

'Where to?' Toni asked.

'The Grand Hotel, of course,' Fletcher laughed. 'Where else?'

Even if he was on the wrong track about the American party, he had earned a few days of comfort, he thought, and relaxed in his seat.

At the hotel, he took a shower and decided to catch a few hours sleep. When he awoke the brilliant sunshine was making the gilt-domed rooms, and whitewashed buildings, which surrounded the harbour of Piraeus, glitter and sparkle. For Fletcher this was as near home as he could ever be. A nomad by profession, he and Spencer used Piraeus and Athens as their base. Spencer from a bungalow in one of the lush suburbs of the capital and Fletcher from wherever it suited his purpose. Fletcher went to the hotel restaurant for breakfast, but the American party was nowhere to be seen. For a while he studied the sea of faces which filled the room and then turned his attention to the newspaper. He wasn't encouraged by what he read. A Turkish aircraft had been shot down by the Russians close to the Black Sea. The Russians claimed that it had violated their territory and the Turks were denying the accusation. This was the second incident which had occurred recently between the Russians and the Turks. The second deliberate flare-up on the part of the Russians. What were they aiming at? Fletcher wondered. Why lower the temperature? He knew the Soviet's tactics as well as his own, and their methods. Whether or not the Turkish plane had violated their territory was a matter of conjecture. It was happening all the time. The decision to make capital out of it, however, was a political one taken at Kremlin level. The Russians had some ulterior plan in mind. The other piece of news which gave Fletcher cause for concern was more pertinent. Abdul Mohmud, a member of the Aden Government, had been assassinated, struck down with a knife as he had returned home from a meeting. His death was being denied by all parties, but tension was mounting. The precarious peace which followed the British withdrawal was in danger of being shattered. But it was not this alone which gave Fletcher cause for anxiety. Mohmud had been a secret friend and admirer of the British. He had been one of their few friends in power. Was that why the man had been so foully murdered? he wondered. Had they found out about him? It didn't make pleasant conjecture.

The delicacy of the International situation stirred Fletcher into action. The Middle East was like a barrel of gunpowder and if a shipment of arms was being negotiated, British Intelligence had to know about it.

67

His first call was to Nico, the proprietor of a small bar close to the waterfront. A bar which Fletcher used as a base and a post office. But Nico also had his own chain of contacts which had served Fletcher well in the past. From Nico's bar he spent the day touring the seaport and the capital spreading his net. He wanted news about the syndicate and news about Kaddir, and he was prepared to pay for it.

When he eventually returned to his hotel it was late in the afternoon. He took a shower, changed, and went in search of the American party. He found them in the lounge bar talking to an Englishman – a tall, rotund, pompous looking man with a red face and a central bald patch to his greying hair, who appeared to commandeer the conversation. In the American party was Carol Marsh, Carl Lipman, the tall man Fletcher had seen at Ali's club, and a small, dumpy man, with close-cropped hair and wearing thick-lensed spectacles. A quiet word with the floor waiter and a quick exchange of a few drachmas and Fletcher had all their names. The Englishman was called Wilson, the tall American – Young, and the small, bespectacled man, Marlow.

Fletcher watched and listened from the background, but as soon as it turned dark he had to leave them. It was time to report to Spencer. He went to Athens by train and from the station made his way discreetly to Spencer's bungalow.

'You're late,' Spencer said gruffly as he admitted him.

'I didn't know we had arranged any particular time,' Fletcher replied evenly, but took note of Spencer's manner. It was an indication that something was up.

'We didn't, but I did,' Spencer growled. 'We are going to a meeting.'

Fletcher didn't inquire further. Spencer wasn't in a communicative mood. He followed him to his garage.

'Keep out of sight,' Spencer said.

Fletcher got into the rear of the car and buried himself in the well-upholstered seat. Spencer drove swiftly out of his drive and on to the road which took them away from Athens to the mountains to the North.

Fletcher remained silent, prepared to let Spencer make the first move.

'You did well, Stephen,' Spencer said eventually, 'but they are on the warpath.' By 'they' Fletcher knew he was referring to London.

'Whom are we meeting?' Fletcher asked.

'Can't give you any details, blast it,' Spencer grumbled, 'except that it's one of them, and Maxwell's crew.'

'He's back is he?' Fletcher asked.

'Yes, arrived yesterday.'

'Empty-handed?'

'No, he got results.' Spencer cursed a passing motorist who had come perilously close to them. 'Don't ask any more questions,' he said. 'We'll soon be there.'

'You're the boss,' Fletcher sighed.

'No, I'm not,' Spencer retorted. 'They are.'

Fletcher half smiled. Spencer liked to be left alone. He didn't like having London breathing down his neck. It made him even more touchy than he normally was.

The road started to wind its way up the wooded slopes of the foothills, and Spencer sat forward in his bucket seat looking for some sign of identification. When he found it, he gave a grunt of satisfaction, and swung the car off the road and over a rough track through the trees. Presently, they came to a large private residence. As Fletcher got out, he saw there were three other cars parked outside the entrance. A light was suddenly shone in his face.

'All right,' Spencer barked. 'He's with me.'

The light was extinguished and the figure brushed past Fletcher.

'Americans?' Fletcher asked, but got no reply.

They were met at the entrance door by a small man, neatly dressed in a plain grey suit and striped tie. He had a pleasant face, with balding hair and innocent blue eyes. He looked a quiet, domesticated businessman, but as Spencer grunted and growled,

Fletcher realized he was the man from London.

The man from London shook Fletcher's hand, but offered no form of introduction.

They were taken into a large, well-lit room, furnished in the contemporary style, with a picture window through which could be seen the lights of the capital. There were two other men in the room – Maxwell and another American who was also not introduced. He was a tall man, with a serious face and a stooped gait.

The man from London commented on the view from the window and then covered it with thick draped curtains. He offered each of his visitors a drink and then got down to business.

'Well, gentlemen, shall we go into the boardroom?' He ushered them into an adjoining room with a large, central, polished table. On a side table stood a ciné projector opposite a wall screen. The man from London glanced at the assembled company seated at the table.

'Three months ago,' he said, 'the British and American Ambassadors in Paris were approached by a group of representatives from the Arab countries, who were in Paris attending a monetary conference. Their approach had no official backing, but it was made with the blessing of various sections of their respective Governments. The gist of the

71

approach was threefold. Firstly, they claimed that the majority of Arab Governments were becoming alarmed at the slow, but strangling grip, the Soviets were getting on their economy and their armed forces. They wanted encouragement from the West for a move in policy towards further alignment with the U.S.A. and Britain. They also wanted a large financial loan from the U.S.A. to bolster their monetary fund, and more Western investments. Finally, they requested that the P.M. makes a personal intervention to bring about a treaty with Israel and the restoration to the Arab countries of their territories now occupied by the Israelis. It was felt that as the U.K. has a long history of dealings in the Middle East they would be considered less controversial than if the U.S.A. intervened.'

The man paused and took a drink from a glass. The four other men sat waiting for him to continue, knowing that they were being given facts known to very few.

'After consultations between London and Washington an unofficial reply was given to the delegation. It was the green light. Create the appropriate internal temperature and we would act. Needless to say, gentlemen, this was a major diplomatic victory for the West. The Soviets have had their eyes on the Middle East from the outset of their Bolshevik revolution, and had almost achieved the first stage of their domination in that area. Now we have the opportunity of stalling them.'

Again he paused, and looked at each man's face in turn.

'But we are in great danger of letting this opportunity slip between our fingers,' he said gravely.

The men remained silent, waiting for him to spell out what they had all come to fear.

'The Soviets were informed of this approach. They were given the full details.' The man sighed. 'Which means that once again we have a traitor in our midst. Unless, of course,' he added brightly, 'one of the delegates is working for the Russians.'

The man raised his eyebrows as if inviting comment. Maxwell spoke up.

'Why should it be one of either party?' he asked. 'If these delegates represented strong factions in their own country, then the field is much broader.'

The man from London smiled.

'It is possible, I agree,' he said, 'but we think otherwise. Immediately London and Washington agreed to go ahead they drafted a term of reference, a sort of step by step sequence of conditions. These were given to the delegates and also sent to each of our Embassies in the Middle East. Needless to say it was given maximum security, which means that not more than three people in each Embassy knew of its existence. Within

73

twenty-four hours of its issue a copy turned up in the Kremlin!'

The last remark brought various forms of reaction from the assembled company. Fletcher grunted, a habit he was prone to doing to cover his embarrassment, or display his disapproval. Maxwell was more vocal. He swore. Spencer growled like a wounded lion and the tall, academic-looking American withdrew a pair of thick-rimmed spectacles from his jacket pocket and started to clean them, furiously, with a white linen handkerchief.

'Each of the Embassies which was informed,' the man continued, 'both British and American, are now undergoing an intensive security check. Until they are cleared they will all be considered a security risk.'

No wonder Spencer was not in the best of spirits, Fletcher thought. Such a situation would hinder him in his work.

'Now that the Russians know what we are up to they have started the necessary counter moves. They intend to both discredit the West and prove to the Arabs that they have the upper-hand in the Middle East. How they intend to do this we do not know.' The man paused and added forcibly, 'Yet.' He took another drink from his glass. 'But we do know that at the moment they appear to have the edge. In the past three months four men have been assassinated. Two in Iraq, one in Jordan, and one yesterday in Aden. All of these men were influential Government people who were supporters of the pro-Western move. It is obvious, gentlemen, that the Soviets are going to unleash a reign of terror on all the various Government heads they suspect, or know, are supporters of the new wind of change.'

'Won't this weaken their cause?' Fletcher asked.

'Yes,' the man replied firmly. 'If it can be proved. But each assassination has been carried out openly in front of people, and by what appears to be local assassins.'

'Appears?' Spencer growled.

'Let us say that the assassins have appeared to be natives, fellahin, or what you have. They could have been disguised, but I rather think not. It is taking a risk. After very close investigation by the Iraquis and Jordanian officials, and I may add by both of our intelligence networks, there is no evidence of any local Soviet agents being involved. Which makes us suspect that they are being imported in especially for these operations.'

Again there was a wave of resentment in the room.

'We also know that Breznov was given the task of strengthening the bonds between the U.A. Republics and the Soviet Union, and as we are all aware, Breznov is both a Soviet diplomat and number two in the K.G.B. On

July 4th Breznov flew into Baghdad, but returned to Moscow on the same day. Whilst in Baghdad he met the Iraqui Defence Minister. He is a pro-communist sympathizer and not one of those who support a move to the West. Unfortunately Breznov's visit was unexpected and we were unable to get any information of what took place at that meeting. On July 5th Breznov flew into Cairo. On the 6th he had a meeting with the Egyptian Foreign Secretary and the Iraqui Defence Minister, who had also flown into Cairo on the 5th. The day after that meeting, Breznov returned to Moscow. On the same day, both the British and American Embassies are given a copy of the report of Breznov's meeting by their respective Intelligence Services. Very good work, gentlemen, but let me give you a word of warning. Think carefully before you use your contacts again, because we believe that the leak was an official one!'

Again Fletcher coughed. All the time he had been dealing with Ali he had felt that something was out of line. It had been too easy.

'Well! I'll be dog-garned,' Maxwell said incredulously.

The man from London made a gesture with his hands.

'Please, gentlemen,' he said. 'Although we believe the leak was intentional, we still believe that what you have got was an authentic copy of the report which was submitted to the President.' He turned to the tall American. 'Isn't that so?

The American put on his spectacles as if he was going to read from a report.

'Yes, that is so,' he said in a polished Yale accent. 'The two reports are identical. They were both taken with the same camera. There are slight movements of position which indicates that whoever took the shots made two separate attempts. We believe that the reports are authentic.'

'So you see, gentlemen, your work was not in vain.' The man from London smiled. 'As to the contents of the report... Well, gentlemen, it contained nothing we didn't know already or would not have found out as a matter of course. Statements of mutual foreign policy between the Soviet Union and the U.A.R.'s. and agreement for the supply of various defensive types of weapons.'

'Which explains why the Egyptians allowed the leak,' a voice said. It was Maxwell.

'If it was the Egyptians,' the man from London retorted pointedly. 'We think it was by the Russians, to distract us from whatever they are up to.' He looked around the assembled company.

'Any comments?' he asked.

'Yes,' Fletcher said in his deep, resonant voice. 'Why send Breznov? What he accomplished could also have been achieved by someone who attracted less attention.'

'Why indeed?' the man sighed. 'I think we have come to the point when we stop giving answers and let you gentlemen get on with it.' He looked meaningly at Spencer who stood up and walked over to the ciné projector. From his pocket he withdrew a reel of film, and mounted it in the projector.

'Breznov was supposed to have left Cairo the day after his meeting with the Egyptian Foreign Secretary,' he said gruffly, 'but he didn't. Someone like Breznov flew out. Breznov remained in Cairo for one further day to meet these two men.'

He threw a switch which started the reel.

'This is the rear entrance to the Soviet Embassy,' he explained. 'These shots were taken at four p.m. on the day Breznov was supposed to have flown to Moscow.' A car drew up outside the gate and a man got out. It was the Iraqui Defence Minister.'The next man is a newcomer,' Spencer said. From another car a man appeared. Spencer froze the film to show the man in full flight from the vehicle to the entrance gate. 'This is our mystery man,' Spencer confessed. 'We are hoping you can help us, David.' He had directed his remark to Maxwell.

Fletcher studied the still on the screen. The man was small, portly, wearing a white linen suit and hat. His features were blurred, but he was unmistakenly of Eastern origin with a round, dark face.

'He was staying at the Carlton Hotel,' Spencer explained, 'under the name of Mohammed Mizar. He had a U.A.R. passport. He left the day after the meeting on a flight for Tehran.'

'Tehran!' Maxwell explained. 'Got him! He is Muzaf Kabul, a member of the Persian Communist Party.'

Spencer gave a satisfied grunt and switched off the lamp.

'Nice work, John,' Maxwell said from across the table.

Spencer retrieved the spool and returned to his seat.

'This Persian, Kabul?' the man from London asked, taking command again. 'What about him?'

The tall American adjusted his spectacles.

'He's from the North of Iran,' he said. 'Comes from peasant stock. Evidently showed promise at school and a well-to-do landowner took him under his wing. Eventually he got a degree at Tehran University. Since then he has moved about. He was sacked from a Government appointment when his political views became known. He can speak several languages fluently and got a job with an International Trading Company.'

The American looked at his colleague, Maxwell.

'Anything else?' he asked.

'Only that he is not one of the Communists' front boys. However, some of our latest reports indicate that he is becoming one of the powers behind the scenes. If the party is ever given official recognition he will be the man they will have to deal with.'

'Thank you, gentlemen,' the man from London said quietly. 'We now know who we are dealing with.' He dropped his head momentarily and then braced himself.

'Gentlemen,' he said in a crisp, but quiet voice, 'we don't know very much, but we know a lot more than we did three days ago. We know the outcome of Breznov's talks at official level. We also know he stayed in Cairo one further evening and had a secret meeting with the Iraqui Defence Minister and a prominent Communist from Persia.' He looked around the assembled group. 'We also know that the Russians are rubbing up the Turks at the diplomatic level. Turkey, Iraq, Persia – somewhere there is a common denominator. The Russians have to do something to restore their prestige before the pro-West advocates get complete control.' He paused. 'My guess is that it is somewhere in the East.'

In the East! Something clinked into place in Fletcher's brain. It was not often that reference was made to the 'East' in Middle East dealings, but he had heard it quite recently. Ali had used the same expression, when he had referred to Kaddir. Kaddir came from the East, and Timovsky had struggled with a name not unlike Kaddir...

'Do you agree?' the man had directed his question to the tall American.

'Russian strategy in the past has been to lower the temperature at the diplomatic level to a cold front before making their move. This at the moment appears to be directed towards Turkey.' The American fingered his spectacles. 'We know that the Russians would like to see our fangs removed from our bases in Eastern Turkey. They probably know that we are negotiating for bases in Persia. We also know that Turkey and Iraq have certain differences. Perhaps they are plotting to put pressure on to Turkey and Persia. It is early days. Our intelligence in the East has had top priority recently and they have not given any indication of trouble.'

Fletcher saw a frown appear on Maxwell's face. The East was one of his responsibilities. Fletcher appreciated how he felt.

The man from London sighed.

'At this stage it is all surmise,' he said regretfully. 'We are not presuming to teach you gentlemen your job. You have given us admirable service. I am sure we can leave this problem with you!'

He stood up and said cheerfully, 'Care for a drink?'

But it was only his counterpart, the tall

American, who accepted the invitation. Together they left the room leaving the three
agents with their problem.

It was Maxwell who spoke first.

'You know, John,' he drawled, 'I must be
getting old. The thoughts of that pension
becomes more attractive every day.'

Fletcher glanced across at the man. His
face looked tired and furrowed. He had
spoken from his heart, Fletcher thought, he
was looking forward to retirement. He felt a
moment of sympathy for the man. He wasn't
young, and the Middle East was not his
home like Spencer and Fletcher. He was an
imported agent. A man who had been sent to
the Middle East when the first American
base in Turkey had been constructed, and
since that day had been responsible for their
intelligence. Fletcher had worked with him
before. He was a good agent, not imaginative
like Spencer, but then Spencer was unique.
Suddenly Fletcher realized how little he
knew about the man. Was he married? Did he
have any family? They were questions you
never asked a man in their line of business,
but Fletcher began to wonder.

'Don't worry, David,' Spencer said in his
gruff manner. 'They have never checkmated
us yet, and they won't this time. We'll beat
this one.'

'Sure,' Maxwell replied. 'The trouble is
each move becomes more difficult to follow.'

He lit a cigarette and studied the picture of the camel on the packet, thoughtfully.

'How do you want to work it?' he asked abruptly.

Fletcher looked at Spencer and caught his eyes. There were things they had to discuss. Matters which could best be said in private. He didn't want to give Maxwell any suspicions until he got Spencer's approval.

Spencer got the message.

'I think we'll sleep on it, David,' he said. 'I want to check through some old reports.'

'Good idea,' Maxwell agreed. 'We have quite a file on that region. There may be something I have overlooked.'

He slid his chair away from the table. 'Well,' he sighed, 'it looks as if I will be hot-footing it back East.'

'Not before we have a talk,' Spencer warned. 'I'll contact you in the usual way.'

'Sure,' Maxwell drawled. 'Now how about that drink?'

'Not for us,' Spencer growled. 'We have to be getting back.'

They left the table and rejoined the other two men, but for Spencer and Fletcher it was only for a short while. The man from London saw them out of the building like a managing director seeing some of his executive staff off his premises after a working visit. But there was a difference. The following morning the man would be gone – back to London. The villa would be handed back to the prominent Greek shipping magnate who befriended the two Western powers. The meeting had never taken place.

Spencer drove swiftly away from the villa. Again Fletcher sat in the dark corner of the rear seat.

'Well,' Spencer said. 'You've got the whole picture now.'

'Is that why you wanted me to be present?' Fletcher asked.

'Yes,' Spencer growled. 'The way things are going, three heads are better than one.' He was including Maxwell. 'I hope you have something for me.'

'Yes, I have,' Fletcher replied and added thoughtfully, 'I only hope it is relevant.'

'Leave it until we get to the bungalow. I could do with a drink.'

At the bungalow they parked the car and retired to Spencer's study. Behind locked doors, they studied a large wall map of the Middle East from two comfortable chairs, and toyed with cut-glass tumblers of iced whisky.

Fletcher related the events which had taken place in Cairo, omitting only his suspicions about the visiting party of Americans.

'So you think Timovsky was trying to say Kaddir?' Spencer asked when he had finished.

'I am not sure,' Fletcher replied truthfully,

'but it was rather similar. Certainly Kad.'

'Kaddir,' Spencer muttered thoughtfully. 'It means nothing to me. You say he is from the East?'

'From the Kandahar region,' Fletcher said. 'That is according to Ali, but he could be lying.'

'More than likely,' Spencer agreed.

'We could always lean on Ali,' Fletcher pointed out.

Spencer looked pensive.

'I think we'll have to, Stephen,' he said. 'I don't damn well like it. The general situation is too delicate. I'll contact Hamilton to take care of Ali. I presume you've got your contacts working here in Athens.'

'Yes, I've put out a wide net. Something will come our way.'

'Take care,' Spencer warned. 'We could get our fingers burned. They play rough.'

Fletcher didn't need any warning. He had brushed with the syndicate before. There was big money involved in their business – very big – and they were out to protect it.

'How do you feel about the suggestion that the opposition have a plant?' he asked.

'Of course they damned well have,' Spencer fumed. 'But that's the job for Security. They'll be arriving tomorrow, poking their noses into everybody's business. Blasted nuisance, but damn it, man, we can't wait until they give the green light. We have to carry on.'

'It could be on the American side,' Fletcher pointed out.

'Yes, they are equally vulnerable.' Spencer looked at him. 'What are you getting at?'

'It's only a long shot,' Fletcher said slowly, 'but remember that cutting we found on Tomovsky?'

'Yes, what of it?'

'We automatically assumed that he was referring to the firms that the Russians were placing orders with. Correct?'

'Correct.'

'But we all know that Timovsky was employed by the K.G.B. He wasn't really interested in trade.'

'So?'

'On the reverse side of the newspaper cutting we found on him was a news item. It referred to the visit to Baghdad of members of the American Peace Corps.'

'The same people who gave the talk at Cairo University?' Spencer asked.

'Yes.'

'Anything else?'

'They arrived the same day as Breznov.'

'And left the same day,' Spencer added. 'They are here in Athens, staying at the Grand.'

'Speaking of hotels,' Fletcher said. 'They were also staying at the Carlton in Cairo.'

Spencer frowned, poured himself another

drink, and frowned again.

Fletcher knew he wasn't enthusiastic.

'Purely a coincidence,' Spencer growled.

'Do you have any other suggestions about who might be helping them?' Fletcher asked, slightly irritated that Spencer should cold-shoulder his suspicions.

'No, I haven't, and I'm not even trying to guess. The field is too wide open. You know how many people could be suspect?'

Fletcher didn't answer. He was well aware that the combined staffs of the British and American Embassies in the Middle East mounted to well over a hundred. It would be a long list.

'I'm more interested in finding out what the Soviets are up to,' Spencer added. 'Once we know that, we'll be able to foil them. Leave the other thing to Security.'

But Fletcher's tenacity wouldn't let him give up. He had a bee in his bonnet about the touring party of Americans, and he wasn't going to be shunted to one side. He got hold of Spencer's pointer and let it rest on the wall chart against the eastern end of Turkey.

'That's where they do most of their work,' he said. 'There.' He touched the map at Lake Van on the edge of the Hakkari Mountains. 'And in Iraq and Persia amongst the tribes people.' He paused and added forcibly. 'In the East!'

'And do you think the C.I.A. aren't watching them?' Spencer asked testily.

'Were we watching the men we lost to the Soviets?' Fletcher retorted. 'Oh! I know it's a long shot, but it's worth following up.' He paused, and added, 'I booked in at the Grand also, to keep an eye on them.'

Spencer looked up sharply and frowned, but he saw the stubbornness in Fletcher's eyes and turned and sat pensively looking at the wall chart. Then, as if on an impulse, he stood up and furrowed through some papers on his desk, until he found what he was looking for. It was a gilt-edged invitation card.

'I think you are on the wrong track,' he growled, 'but since you are so determined to pursue it – this might help.'

He handed Fletcher the card. It was an invitation to a reception to be held the following evening, at the American Club, to meet Dr Bradshaw and his colleagues.

Fletcher smiled. 'Thanks,' he said, 'it will make a nice change. What line would you suggest?'

'I'll phone Peekas first thing in the morning,' Spencer replied.

Fletcher nodded his head, approvingly. Peekas was the editor of a weekly magazine and they had used his services before with success. He was an old colleague of Spencer's from the war days, when they had worked together on Middle East Intelligence. Their friendship had often been instrumental in providing a cover for some of Spencer's activities. Tomorrow would be no different. Peekas would again agree to Fletcher becoming one of his staff.

Fletcher felt much better. He knew Spencer wasn't keen, but at least he wasn't trying to hinder him.

They sat talking for a while longer, exhausting various possible lines of thought, but without reaching any definite conclusions. Finally, they made arrangements to meet in Peekas' office, during the morning following the reception, and Fletcher returned to Piraeus.

He called in at Nico's bar, but there was nothing to report. The fish was still at large.

Chapter Four

'Certainly, old boy, we can get the stuff.' The pseudo, polished accent, carried across the room and attracted Fletcher's attention by its contrast with the American accents which monopolised the hub of conversations. Fletcher glanced at the owner of the voice. It was the pompous, red-faced Englishman he had seen in the hotel with the American party. He was talking to Lipman, and his stance and manner gave the impression that he was well accustomed to attending such functions.

A waiter with a tray of drinks interrupted Fletcher's study of the man. Fletcher accepted a drink and looked around the brightly-lit, crowded reception. He recognized some of the British and American Embassy staff and the party of Peace Corps members he had seen at Cairo University. He also saw Maxwell in the far corner deep in conversation with one of their Military Attaches.

Fletcher had just arrived at the reception. He had been introduced to Dr Bradshaw by one of the staff from the Embassy and had spent a few minutes in the Doctor's company. No mention had been made by either

91

Fletcher or the Doctor, to the fact that they had flown from Cairo, the previous day, on the same flight, but Fletcher was quick to detect a look of uncertainty on the Doctor's face during their introduction. A look which had suggested to Fletcher that the Doctor was trying to put a place and name tag on him! When the Doctor had been called away to meet another guest, Fletcher had crossed over to a photographic display showing the work carried out by the Peace Corps. It was there that the Englishman's voice had attracted his attention.

He noticed that Carol Marsh, who was also at the display, had finished explaining certain aspects of their work to a group of Greek officials and he moved towards her. Intentionally he allowed himself to bump into her, spilling his drink.

'Sorry,' he said, quickly bringing out his handkerchief.

'It's quite all right,' she smiled. 'It missed me.'

'That's a relief,' he smiled back at her. 'I should hate to ruin such a charming dress.'

She accepted the compliment with a faint look of amusement.

'Have we met before?' she asked. 'Your face is familiar.'

'I'm afraid not,' Fletcher replied, 'although I understand we are both staying at the same hotel. I am Stefan Fettos.' He hoped she didn't remember him from anywhere else.

'Dr Carol Marsh,' she explained.

They shook hands. She was much older than he had originally thought. Her face was beginning to show the signs that women tried so hard to camouflage. But she was nevertheless attractive. She had a very dark skin and jet-black hair which made her look more Eastern than American. Her figure wasn't too bad either, he thought.

'You speak very good English,' she said. Her accent was less pronounced that most Americans he had met. 'What line of business are you in?'

'Journalism,' Fletcher explained, and handed her his specially printed card which he used on such occasions. She examined it and handed it back to him.

'My editor is very interested in your work,' he said. 'He is considering doing an article about it.'

'Is he?' she asked. 'Then let me explain these photographs to you.'

She turned to the display.

'This one shows a new school which we built in Eastern Turkey,' she said pointing to one of the photographs. 'And this is an irrigation scheme we installed in a small town near Lake Van.'

She went from photograph to photograph proudly pointing out their achievements. Fletcher was genuinely impressed.

A lot of the photographs had been taken in the remote parts of Turkey and Iraq – a region of rugged geography and primitive conditions.

'How do you overcome the language difficulties?' he asked.

'Ah! they are difficulties, I agree,' she said seriously. 'However, some of us can speak Kermanji.'

Kermanji! Fletcher's pulse quickened. My God! he thought, that was it! That was the tongue the Arab had cried out in, when he had threatened him with the knife! Kermanji, the language of the Kurdish tribes who lived in the mountainous region which bordered Turkey, Iraq and Persia! A flood of thought raced through his brain. The Kurds were a tall, narrow-faced race, with Arabic features. Many of them from the North were fair skinned and blue eyed, whilst those from the South were much darker. The man who had knifed Timovsky was fair haired! He could have been one of them! But many others could pass unnoticed in any Middle East capital. Was this the common denominator?

Carol Marsh continued to describe the various photographs, but Fletcher had other thoughts. The Kurds had long since been a thorn in the flesh to the three countries which bordered the Soviet Union. An independent Kurdistan had first been proposed after the First World War, but it had not come to fruition, and the Kurdish rebellion of 1925 had resulted in a blood-bath. The rebellion had been put down, but a seething resentment still lingered. And hadn't the Russians again proposed an independent Kurdistan in 1945?

'If your editor wants a story you should come and visit us in the field,' Carol Marsh said.

'Where is that?' Fletcher asked, putting his thoughts temporarily to the back of his mind.

'Oh, near Lake Van in Eastern Turkey.'

'Amongst the Kurds?' Fletcher asked.

'Yes, that's right.'

'It sounds a good idea,' he said and meant it.

'Let me introduce you to some of our other workers.'

She led him over to Carl Lipman, who was talking to a Greek Army officer. After she had introduced Fletcher, she and the Greek moved on, leaving Fletcher alone with Lipman.

'Have you been out here very long?' Fletcher asked.

Lipman's poker face looked straight at Fletcher, but he didn't reply straight away. Fletcher wondered why.

'No,' he said finally. 'I came out last fall.'

'This is your first round trip?' Fletcher persisted.

'No, I have done three tours,' Lipman replied, but didn't enlarge upon his statement. 'And you, Mr Fettos. Do you travel far?'

'Round and about,' Fletcher said.

'How long have you worked for your magazine?'

Fletcher gave him the set answer which he knew Peekas would confirm.

'You will know our P.R.O.?' Lipman asked.

Fletcher knew, well enough, that he referred to Greg Young, the tall, fresh-faced American, he had seen in Ali's Club in Cairo, but he decided to act dumb.

'I'm afraid I don't,' he lied. 'Is he here?'

'That's him across there talking to Vince Marlow our agricultural expert. Come, I'll introduce you.'

Lipman was being very helpful, Fletcher thought, as he followed him to where the two men were standing.

Lipman made the introductions. Young responded to the handshake with a firm grip, but Marlow just held out a limp, podgy hand. Young was from one of the Southern States, and he spoke in a slow, drawling accent, which gave a misleading impression of the man's ability. His speech may have been slow and soft but his questions and flashing eyes indicated a sharp brain. He showed a great deal of interest in Fletcher's supposed role of a journalist, and even more in the political situation at present existing in Greece, and the series of confrontations which were taking place between Greece and Turkey. Marlow was less talkative. He was a northerner from Detroit, brought up against an industrial background and had spent most of his years in the Far East giving advice on agricultural methods. His beady eyes, enlarged behind thick-lensed spectacles, seemed trained on Fletcher, as if trying to penetrate his innermost thoughts.

Lipman soon left them, but Fletcher noticed he often glanced in their direction.

'So your editor is interested in running a series on us, is he?' Young asked.

'Yes,' Fletcher agreed, 'but I would like to get hold of some fresh material.'

'Come into the field,' Marlow said. 'That's the only place you'll get that.'

'Sure,' Young drawled. 'We are going into the field ourselves, for a spell, after we get back to Ankara. Why don't you join us?'

'Eastern Turkey?' Fletcher asked.

'Yes, we work from a central base at Kiran near Lake Van,' Marlow explained.

In the heart of Kurdish territory, Fletcher thought. If anything was being planned for the Kurds that's where it would take place.

'I'm sure you would find it interesting,' Young added in his lazy accent.

Very, Fletcher thought, and wondered whether the smile on Young's face hid any deeper thoughts.

'It sounds a good idea,' Fletcher said with feigned enthusiasm, 'I'll certainly put it to my editor. It's a long time since we sent anyone to the Eastern regions of Turkey.'

'Someone going to Eastern Turkey?' a voice asked. Fletcher didn't need to look around to see its owner. It was the Englishman he had previously overheard.

'Hullo, Mr Wilson,' Young said warmly. 'Come and join us.'

The Englishman strolled into their midst with an air of condescension, and a smile upon his face that irritated Fletcher.

'Did I hear someone say that they were going East?' he asked, in his loud voice.

'Yes, Mr Fettos is thinking of doing so,' Marlow explained.

'Fettos? Have we met?'

'No,' Fletcher responded. 'I would have remembered.'

Marlow introduced Wilson, and Fletcher patiently explained the reason for his remark about visiting Eastern Turkey. Wilson soon lost interest, however, and proceeded to discuss some recent business transaction he had negotiated with the Americans. Fletcher soon gathered that he represented a firm which dealt with supplies and was also made aware, at an early stage, of the man's high position in his organization.

Across the room Fletcher caught Maxwell's eye. He was talking to Carol Marsh and a

98

group of Greek Army officers. There was a fractional movement of Maxwell's eyes towards the open french doors. Shortly after, Fletcher saw Maxwell disengage himself from his party and stroll out of the room, to the patio where several guests had gathered.

Fletcher politely excused himself, but as Wilson was starting to hold forth on some past experience, and the two Americans appeared to be under his spell, his departure was barely noticed.

On the patio, Fletcher hesitated, accepted a drink from a waiter, and listened to a Greek official pointing out the various temples of the Acropolis which were illuminated in the distance.

Satisfied that no one was watching him, he walked slowly along the dimly-lit path through the scented garden.

He hadn't gone far when Maxwell joined him.

'I got a message from Spencer today. He told me about Kaddir, and also of your suspicions,' Maxwell whispered.

'What do you think?' Fletcher asked.

'Kaddir could be very dangerous,' Maxwell said. 'If he is in the big league. We can't afford to ignore him.'

'And the other business?'

Maxwell shrugged.

'I'm inclined to go along with Spencer,' he said.

But he wasn't as forceful as Spencer, Fletcher thought. That at least was hopeful.

'We've kept a close watch on them,' Maxwell added. 'That's why I am here.'

'Why is that necessary?' Fletcher asked.

'We got a signal from Washington, a few weeks ago, to keep Marlow and Young under surveillance until they cleared certain irregularities.'

'What sort of irregularities?'

'They didn't say, they never do. When we accept applicants for the Corps they are given the normal vetting, but it is not a thorough business. It is only when they are promoted to become part of the Embassy staff that they get the full treatment.'

'I see,' Fletcher said.

Maxwell stopped in his tracks.

'I thought I heard someone,' he said in a hushed tone.

They both stood and listened, but other than the customary insect noises there was nothing to be heard.

'Must have been mistaken,' Maxwell grunted, and got back to the matter in hand. 'Young and Marlow left the field four months ago for a spell in Ankara. Consequently they were given the full security check. Marsh was given a full clearance about ten months ago. The other two still have question-marks beside their names.'

Young and Marlow! Fletcher wondered

about the two men. Young, the idealist who hid his true identity behind his lazy southern manner, and Marlow, the man who had lived with the backward and underdeveloped people for the past twenty years. They were both likely suckers for the Communist line.

'What about Dr Bradshaw and Lipman?'

'Dr Bradshaw was appointed by the State Department,' Maxwell grunted, 'but he has been cleared. As for Lipman? He came direct from Washington to do his job. He wasn't from the field, so Washington cleared him before he left.'

'What is his job?'

'He is their Q man. Responsible for distribution of all supplies. He's on loan from a large concern in the mid-West.'

'Temporary?' Fletch asked. 'Is this customary?'

'Yes, a large percentage only join for a year or two. It's only people like Marsh and Marlow who make a career of it.'

'Could Washington be wrong? About Lipman?'

'It has been known,' Maxwell agreed, 'but it's unlikely. What do you have in mind?'

'Just curiosity,' Fletcher said. He had nothing to go on. Only an impression about Lipman that could be way off course.

'That's the reason I have been following them around,' Maxwell explained.

'Did anything turn up?'

'It's difficult to say,' Maxwell grumbled. 'Both of them gave me the slip at the hotel in Cairo, and now we find that Kabul was staying there also.'

'You didn't see Kabul at the hotel?' Fletcher asked.

'Hell, no. The first I knew was from that film.'

'And after they leave here they are returning to Eastern Turkey?'

Maxwell stopped walking and turned to him.

'Say, what's your angle?' he asked quietly.

'It's a long shot,' Fletcher said, 'but supposing the Russians have recruited a number of Kurds to act as agents for them. Could you pick them out amongst the other dark faces?'

'Kurds!' Maxwell exclaimed. 'Kurds!' The question had taken him by surprise. His brow became furrowed in a frown. 'It would be difficult,' he said. 'Unless they came from the North – they can be quite fair.'

'The man who killed Timovsky was fair and yet looked like an Arab.'

'Hell, why should they help the Soviets?' Maxwell asked, but didn't wait for an answer. 'Have you spoken to Spencer about this?'

'Not yet, why?'

'I handed some reports over to him which we received last month from that region. There was mention of an Iraqui move for an independent Kurdistan. Nobody took it seriously, but if you are right…'

He didn't finish his sentence, but Fletcher could almost read his mind.

'I wonder,' Maxwell said pensively. 'There's a lot of money invested in those bases of ours and they are close to those mountains.'

'You think we could be on to something?' Fletcher asked.

'Your guess is as good as mine,' Maxwell whispered, 'but it has been a potential flash-spot since the 1925 rebellion. If the Kurds are working for the Soviets they'll be wanting something in return. We can't afford to overlook the possibility. We have a number of contacts in the region of Kiran. It might be worth a visit.'

'What about the party from the Corps.'

'I'll chase up Washington tonight,' Maxwell growled. 'If they have found out anything about Young or Marlow, I'll … wait.' He stopped mid-sentence and stood quite still. A faint crackle from a moving branch broke the silence.

Maxwell touched Fletcher's arm, and he silently told him to carry on along the path and he would go into the bushes. He withdrew a revolver and slipped into the shrubbery. Fletcher continued along the path and then decided to follow Maxwell. If there was someone there, two of them had a better chance of finding him than one. As he turned a flash of steel shot past his face and with a thud buried itself in the trunk of a nearby tree! For a second Fletcher froze, but quickly got over the shock.

Furiously he leapt into the bushes. Someone had tried to kill him! If he hadn't turned at that particular moment the dagger would be sticking in some part of his anatomy! He heard Maxwell cry out and he crashed his way through the bushes determined to get to grips with whoever had thrown that dagger. Maxwell was getting up from the ground. Fletcher didn't help him, he wanted his hands on his would-be murderer. He came to the lawn, and saw a figure in the distance disappearing into the darkness. He was too far away for Fletcher to hope to catch him. Thoughtfully he joined Maxwell. That was the second attempt on his life. Why were the Russians going to such limits to try and get rid of him? Was he beginning to worry them?

'Thank God you are all right,' Maxwell said. 'Any idea who your friend is?'

'He'll be working for the opposition,' Fletcher growled.

'Or the syndicate,' Maxwell added. 'They don't play about.'

'Perhaps,' Fletcher said, but wasn't convinced. It was early days for them. 'Did you see his face?'

'Dark, looked like a Greek,' Maxwell explained, 'but he can handle himself. I thought

I had him.'

'He'll be a professional,' Fletcher said. 'There are plenty about.'

He was going to have to be extra cautious, he thought, and felt a little uneasy at his narrow escape.

'Let's get back and have a drink,' Maxwell sighed. 'I need one.'

'And me,' Fletcher added with feeling.

They parted company. Fletcher went first and rejoined the guests on the patio. Lipman was there and also Carol Marsh.

Fletcher collected a drink and glanced into the reception room. He couldn't see either Young or Marlow, or the extrovert Englishman, but Dr Bradshaw smiled at him from across the room.

'You been in the bushes?' It was Lipman.

'I wandered off the track,' Fletcher said lightly, and brushed his jacket.

'Are the drinks so strong?' Lipman joked.

From the corner of his eye, Fletcher saw Maxwell rejoin the party. He also saw Marlow re-appear and join Carol Marsh. She seemed to have her eyes on Dr Bradshaw.

Fletcher let Lipman's remark ride.

'Still thinking of coming East?' Lipman asked.

Fletcher turned his attention back to the man beside him, and wondered if there had been any particular significance in his choice of words. It was almost as if he had known what had just taken place.

'More so than ever now,' Fletcher said, pan-faced. 'I hope I can persuade my editor.'

'Tell him that you will bring back some very surprising pictures,' Lipman smiled.

'Yes,' Fletcher said. 'I will.'

The two men stood talking for several minutes and Fletcher got the impression Lipman was pumping him. The American was reluctant to talk about himself, or his work, and kept bringing the conversation around to Fletcher's interests. It was as if the two men were having a verbal joust. Finally, Fletcher decided it was time to leave. The reception had thinned out and he noticed Maxwell had also left. He had a last word with Carol Marsh and suggested that, as they were all staying at the same hotel, she had breakfast with him. She politely turned him down and suggested he joined their party instead. This suited Fletcher even better. The reception had done nothing to dispel the misgivings he had about the American party, and the more he got to know them the better it would be. He shook hands with Dr Bradshaw and left the reception.

Outside the club, Toni was waiting for him in his cab. His friendly face was a welcome sight. They returned to Piraeus and Fletcher again went to Nico's bar. This time Nico had some news. Kaddir and his niece had arrived! They had been seen entering the seaport from one of the ferry boats which toured the islands close to the mainland.

'Ferry boat,' Fletcher muttered thoughtfully after the Greek had tod him. That meant that Kaddir had his own means of transport to the islands, either a boat or a 'plane.

'Where are they staying?' he asked.

The Greek gave him the address of a villa in the suburbs of the city. Fletcher knew the area. It was a quiet, respectable district of expensive villas.

'What about our gun-running friends?' he asked. 'Any news?'

The Greek squashed his half-smoked cigarillo into an ashtray and scowled.

'They are as secretive as the Mafia,' he snarled, 'and as dangerous.'

Which meant they were unlikely to get to know anything about their movements at Nico's level, Fletcher thought. His only hope was through Kaddir – or Ali. Perhaps Spencer had heard from Hamilton.

'Keep a watch on the villa,' he said. 'Night and day. I want to know immediately this Kaddir makes a move or is contacted. You can get me at the hotel, or through Toni.'

Nico nodded his head understandingly. Fletcher withdrew a roll of money which quickly found its way into the Greek's pocket, and then returned thoughtfully to his hotel. Was he on the right lines? he wondered.

107

Were the Kurds the common denominator? Were they being recruited to unleash a reign of terror amongst pro-Western Government officials? The man who had attacked him in Cairo had cried out in Kermanji, of that he was now certain. That made him a Kurd, and so probably was Kaddir – and Kaddir was purchasing weapons! The sooner he discussed it with Spencer, the better. Spencer kept himself well informed of the mood of the various tribespeople. He would know if anything was in the wind.

In his hotel bedroom Fletcher took a number of precautions in case his would-be murderer returned. If they were so desperate to get him out of the way, they would try again. It didn't make him feel any happier.

Chapter Five

Fletcher had a trouble-free night, but the morning newspaper headlines showed that the assassin's hand had been active elsewhere. A prominent Turkish-Cypriot had been shot dead. The Greek Cypriots were denying that they had anything to do with the incident, but the Turkish students in Ankara showed their disbelief by demanding physical retaliation. Once again Turkey and Greece were looking at each other from behind gun-sights. Once again the island of Cyprus was at flashpoint. It was becoming an almost regular occurrence, but it only needed one false move, or decision, to start a shooting war. On this occasion there was the added flavour of a Russian warning. In the past she had not been so vocal on the Cyprus dispute, but now she considered it opportune to make herself heard. It was a short statement, but pertinent. She warned Turkey not to take any hasty action, and pointed out the close proximity of the Russian fleet. Once again it was a diplomatic rebuff for the Turks.

As Fletcher read the news he could almost feel Spencer's wrath. Events were occurring fast and they still had no break through – except for his own suspicions. If only he had more concrete evidence.

When he entered the restaurant for breakfast, he saw the American party sitting by the window. Carl Lipman however, was at a separate table with the Englishman, Wilson. Fletcher walked over to them. Carol Marsh smiled a welcome, Marlow grunted from behind his newspaper, and Greg Young made room for him to sit at their table. If the two men were surprised to see him staying at the hotel, they didn't show it, and Fletcher presumed Carol Marsh had pre-warned them. Fletcher embarked upon a review of the latest news, but got little response. Carol Marsh listened, but didn't pass comment. Young, on this occasion, appeared slightly embarrassed at being drawn into a political discussion, and Fletcher wondered if Carol Marsh's presence had anything to do with it. He could almost sense their relief when Wilson and Lipman stopped at the table on their way out of the restaurant.

'Well, Carol, my dear, Carl and I have everything tied up,' Wilson said in his pompous manner from behind a self-satisfied smile. 'We will deliver the stuff to your camp.'

Carol Marsh thanked him, and for a few minutes they discussed one or two details. Fletcher ate his breakfast and listened intently. Wilson was arranging a supply of medical drugs and vaccine for Carol Marsh. The delivery was coming from Iraq to the American base near Lake Van. It was for an expedition Carol Marsh was making into some of the more remote parts of the region. An expedition which Fletcher thought it might be worth joining, and made a mental note to tackle Spencer about it.

'In case I don't see you all tomorrow morning,' Wilson said, 'I wish you a good day and a pleasant trip back to Ankara.'

'Aren't you flying out with us tomorrow?' Young asked.

'No,' Wilson beamed. 'If I get through my business today I will take an earlier flight. Possibly the eight o'clock plane.' He turned to Fletcher. 'It appears all these good people are dining out tonight. How about you and me having dinner together?'

The request took Fletcher by surprise and irritated him because he hadn't a satisfactory excuse for declining. He wanted to be in the hotel so that Nico could contact him, but he wasn't attracted to Wilson's company.

'Certainly,' he replied. 'Nine o'clock in the bar?'

'See you then.'

Wilson left the room with Lipman. Young and Marlow soon followed them.

'You didn't really want to dine with Wilson, this evening, did you?' Carol Marsh asked when they were alone. There was a smile on her face.

'Did it show?' Fletcher asked.

'He wouldn't have noticed,' she said. 'He can be very pompous, but he is also very efficient.'

'So he keeps telling everyone,' Fletcher said dryly.

'Are you serious about coming East?' Carol Marsh asked, changing the subject.

'One hundred per cent,' Fletcher replied. 'In fact I am going to put it to my editor this morning. Why do you ask?'

She shrugged and collected her handbag and belongings.

'There is something about you that puzzles me,' she said seriously, but quickly added, 'Please don't misunderstand me. I am not trying to be rude.'

'Just truthful,' Fletcher smiled.

'See, you haven't even scorned my remark,' she said.

'It flatters me that you have even given me a thought,' he said lightly. 'I would hate to disappoint you. However, if you tell me what puzzles you, perhaps I can ease your mind.'

'That's what worries me,' she said seriously. 'I can't quite put my finger on it.'

'When you do, you will let me know.'

She stood up.

'I certainly will,' she said and held out her hand. She had a firm grip.

'I hope we will meet again,' he said.

'I think we will,' she smiled back at him.

Fletcher watched her leave the room. She was a shrewd, intelligent woman, with an uncanny intuition. She was also damned attractive – rare qualities in any woman. He wondered why she had never married, and decided to ask Maxwell.

After leaving the restaurant Fletcher took a leisurely look at the newspaper again in the lounge, and checked with the desk clerk that there were no messages for him. He then took the train into Athens and went openly to the offices of his newly-appointed employer.

An attractive Greek girl greeted him at the reception counter as if she was expecting him, and ushered him into Peekas' office. Inside was the olive-skinned, grey-haired, wiry Greek, and Spencer. Spencer sat on a straight-backed chair, his hands resting on a walking-stick, and his red face looking as if it was about to burst a blood vessel.

'Good morning, gentlemen,' Fletcher said cheerfully, and sat under the ceiling fan.

'What's good about it?' Spencer growled.

Peekas looked as if he had failed to make the deadline on his last issue.

'Cyprus?' Fletcher asked.

'Amongst other things.'

Spencer wiped his brow.

'Take a look for yourself,' he said.

Fletcher went to the teleprinter and

examined the latest news flashes. The Greek Government had rejected the Turkish note. There was more rioting in Ankara and Istanbul. The Russian fleet had been sighted off one of the Greek islands. But the last flash had been the one that had sent Spencer's blood boiling – an aircraft carrying a special envoy to Turkey from the U.S.A. had blown up and crashed into the Aegean Sea.

Fletcher replaced the tapes on the table and sat down again.

'If that 'plane had been sabotaged, someone was very quick off the mark,' Spencer growled. 'The decision was only made an hour before it took off. I was with the Ambassador when he spoke to the American Embassy.'

'You are only assuming sabotage,' Fletcher said without conviction. 'It could have been other causes.'

'Bah!' Spencer fumed, showing his contempt for Fletcher's remark. 'That was sabotage – by the damned Russians, and so was that assassination on Cyprus. They are stirring it up again.'

'If we know that, why don't the Turks?'

'Because we haven't told them,' Spencer snapped. 'They wouldn't believe us. We need proof.'

'Has Maxwell seen you?' Fletcher asked.

'Yes, but only for a second before he went charging off to Turkey. Said you would tell

me all about it.'

Maxwell had taken him that seriously, Fletcher thought. It was encouraging.

'Also told me to tell you that he hadn't received any word back from Washington,' Spencer added.

'That's a pity,' Fletcher said ruefully.

'What's it all about?'

Fletcher explained what Maxwell had told him, the previous evening, about Young and Marlow. He also told them of the attempt on his life and of Kaddir's arrival.

Spencer looked thoughtful when he had finished.

'You must be on to something,' he growled. 'Someone is worried. I'd better chase up this business about Young and Marlow with Washington.' He mopped the perspiration from his face. 'Now why has David suddenly gone East?'

Fletcher gave a wry smile. He wondered if Spencer would be as enthusiastic as Maxwell.

'When I was in Cairo I was attacked by what I thought was an Egyptian. But he didn't speak Arabic. He spoke Kermanji!'

'A Kurd?' Spencer asked sharply.

'He could have been,' Fletcher said eagerly. 'And so could the man who knifed Timovsky. I remember being puzzled by his fair features, but a lot of Kurds are fair.'

'From the north,' Peekas explained. 'The

southern Kurds are more Arabic.'

Fletcher leant forward.

'Don't you see it?' he asked hopefully. 'The tribespeople who live in the mountains are the common denominator between Turkey, Iraq and Persia and the Soviet Union. Now supposing the Russians have recruited some of them to work for them. Who could pick them out as Kurds?'

'Haven't the Kurds only recently entered into negotiations with the Turkish Government for more autonomy? Peekas asked quietly.

'They have put forward a number of proposals which the Turkish Government are considering,' Spencer said seriously. 'The Kurds have been very active in the past few months lobbying the various Middle East countries for support to their cause.'

'Then why spoil their chances by working for the Russians?' Peekas asked.

'Why indeed?' Spencer growled and added, 'But it only takes one match to light a fire.' He turned to Peekas.

'Let's have a look at the map,' he barked, as if the Greek was still under his command.

Peekas produced a map of the Middle East and spread it over the table. Spencer's finger pointed to the dark brown colouring of the Hakkari Mountains, part of the range of mountains which ran from the Black Sea to the Himalayas. His finger moved and pointed to three locations close to the lighter brown shade of colouring.

'American bases,' he growled. 'If the Russians can get control of these mountains, the Americans might as well go home.' He clenched his fist and thumped the table. 'You've hit the nail on the head, Stephen,' he said. 'Kurds, Lurs, Bakhtiaris. They are all ripe for rebellion. The Russians have had their greedy eyes on these mountains for many a year. Now it looks as if they are going to make their move before it is too late. Before the Kurds settle their differences with the Turks.'

'With Arab support and a Persian demonstration of sympathy?' Fletcher asked.

'Precisely,' Spencer scowled. 'What's the background, Peekas?'

The Greek crossed over to a wall cabinet which displayed bound copies of his magazine from its first issue in 1906. He selected three books from the cabinet and returned to his desk. For a few seconds he sat in deep thought.

'The Kurds were wooed into taking sides in the '14–18 War,' he said quietly, 'but they refused. The Nestorians, who shared the mountains with the Kurds, took sides with the Russians. When the Russians made their peace with the Germans in 1916 many Nestorians fled into the Soviet Union and most of their settlements were taken over by the

Kurds. In 1918 there was a strong national-istic move for an independent Kurdistan. There was a treaty of Sèvres and Lausanne which provided for the creation of an independent Kurdistan, but owing to the Turkish military revival it remained a dead letter. In 1922, Sheik Mahmund proclaimed himself King of Kurdistan, but his reign was short-lived. In 1925 there was open rebellion, which the Turks put down in no uncertain manner. In Persia it was very much the same story. Riza Shah, the ruler, tried to impose his will on the Kurds, which caused resentment, especially amongst the Kushgai tribe of Kurds. In 1944–45 the Kurds set up a Republic in Mahabad with Russian support. The Persians took their case to the Security Council and eventually broke up the Republic. In 1946, after Riza Shah had abdicated, the Kurds, led by the Kushgais, rose up against the regime, but the Persians quelled the uprising in the same manner as the Turks had done. The tribes fled from the Persian border and moved further into the mountains, probably close to the Turko-Soviet border. The Kushgais are a political force to be considered. They have large numbers and are greatly respected by the other Kurdish tribes. Also by the Lurs and Bakhtiaris.'

He opened one of the stiff-backed books. 'Here are some pictures,' he said.

Spencer and Fletcher stood over the Greek and looked at the photographs. They showed various aspects of the Kurds turbulent history following the first and second world wars.

One of the photographs held Fletcher's attention. It was of a group of Kurds in their national costume, not the flat-capped dress Ataturk had influenced upon them. They were dressed in turbans and flowing robes, and heavily armed. One of them was a young, slim, narrow-faced man, with a fertile beard. But his eyes had a familiar look about them.

'That is Serif Kahn,' Peekas explained pointing to a strong-faced, proud-looking man, who stood in the centre of the group. 'He was one of the leaders of the tribe at the time of the 1946 rebellion.'

'Who is the man with the beard?' Fletcher asked.

'It's difficult to say,' Peekas said. 'It could have been one of his sons, he had two.'

Fletcher studied the picture thoughtfully. The man had the look of Kaddir about him, but he couldn't be certain. The beard made it difficult to distinguish his features.

'Are there any more photographs of him?' he asked.

Peekas scanned through several pages, but drew a blank.

''Fraid not,' he said.

'What happened to him?' Fletcher asked.

'Probably fled with the rest of his family.'

'Into Turkey or the Soviet Union?' Fletcher muttered.

'If they didn't go into the Soviet Union they would go close to it.'

Spencer stood upright and breathed heavily.

'I think you had better join Maxwell,' he said to Fletcher.

'What about Kaddir?' Fletcher asked. 'According to Ali, he comes from the Kandahar region, but he could also be a Kurd.'

'I haven't forgotten about him,' Spencer growled. 'He's tied up with it somewhere. He worries me.'

'Any news from Hamilton?' Fletcher asked.

'Yes,' Spencer frowned. 'Ali is dead.'

'Dead!'

'He was found shot in the head the morning after you left.'

'Somebody didn't waste any time,' Fletcher muttered. There was only Kaddir now.

'You've got a watch on the villa?' Spencer asked.

'Yes,' Fletcher replied. 'As soon as he makes a move I'll take over. How long do you want me to stay with it?'

Spencer studied the floor. He saw only too clearly the potential danger of another Kurdish uprising. On the other hand he saw the need to be kept informed of any move of the International syndicate. They were a cancerous organization who sold weapons as if they were toys. They started wars as an everyday part of their business. They were a scourge of society, and Spencer could not afford to ignore their presence in Piraeus. Nor could he pass over an opportunity to get any lead into their chain of command, and Kaddir was their only link.

'Give it another twenty-four hours,' he said. 'If nothing breaks, join Maxwell, and I'll put a watch on the villa. If necessary we can use a bit of pressure on Kaddir.'

'How do I contact Maxwell?'

'He's in the Hakkari area. There is a cobbler called Zarb in Kiran. He will get you in touch with Maxwell.'

'Kiran,' Fletcher said thoughtfully. 'The American party are flying to Ankara tomorrow and then travelling to Kiran on Friday. Why don't I join them? We have a ready-made excuse.'

Spencer looked at Peekas.

'Is it all right with you?' he asked.

'Certainly,' Peekas smiled. 'So long as you take a camera and bring back some photographs.'

'I am told I should get some very interesting photographs,' Fletcher said recalling Lipman's remark.

'There was an American asking for you this morning,' Peekas said. 'He 'phoned just

121

before you arrived. Gina handled him without difficulty. He wouldn't leave a name. He had a pronounced accent.'

Young, thought Fletcher. He had the pronounced drawl. Why should he 'phone? Was he checking up?

'If there are any other calls, let me know,' Fletcher said. It could have been someone impersonating the American, he thought, it wouldn't have been very difficult. But someone was interested in his story.

'Keep in touch with me,' Spencer ordered, interrupting Fletcher's thoughts.

'Where will you be this evening?'

'In the Embassy, entertaining your American friends. You can get me on the special line.' Spencer leant heavily on his stick and scowled. The thought of having to dine at the Embassy didn't appeal to him. There was more urgent matters to attend to.

Soon after, the three men parted company. Fletcher made a call on a contact in Greek Security with the hope of getting some information about the gun-running syndicate, but without success. They were well aware of its existence within their midst, but had no lead into its organization. In Piraeus, however, he got his first report from Nico. Kaddir's niece, Reba, and one of the men, had left the villa and were at the Acropolis, sightseeing. But Kaddir had not left the villa and had not received any visitors. Fletcher wasn't particularly interested in the girl. She was an innocent camouflage for Kaddir. He decided to leave her to the treasures of the antiquity and wait for Kaddir to make his move.

By evening the girl had returned to the villa, but there had been no move by Kaddir. But Fletcher knew well enough that the underworld was nocturnal and they wouldn't make Kaddir wait longer than necessary.

At nine p.m. Fletcher went in search of the Englishman, Wilson, resigned to having to spend a short while in his company. But there was no Wilson in the cocktail bar. Instead a note was handed to Fletcher. It was from Wilson apologizing for his absence. He had decided to take an earlier flight and was flying to Baghdad at ten o'clock that evening. Somewhat relieved Fletcher went into the dining saloon. He had no sooner taken his seat when he was called to the telephone. It was Nico. Kaddir had a visitor! A man had arrived in a car. Who he was or what he looked like was not known. He had arrived a few minutes earlier. Fletcher didn't waste any time. He had to know more about this man and what his business was. Hurriedly he picked up a taxi outside the hotel and was soon in the vicinity of the villa.

He found the villa in a quiet, tree-lined avenue. It was surrounded by a stone wall. He looked at the dark shadows for Nico's man, and was not surprised when he failed to see him. He made a quick decision to take a closer look at the villa, and scaled the wall and dropped gently in amongst the bushes. For a few seconds he stood quite still, in the bright moonlight, listening to the various insect noises. He felt in his pocket and reassured himself that his automatic was handy, and moved slowly through the shrubbery. He soon saw the villa. It was a large L-shaped bungalow with a tiled verandah. A gravel driveway ran past the verandah and a grey saloon car was parked close to the shrubbery.

Stealthily Fletcher crept through the bushes until he came to the driveway. The verandah was directly in front of him. Several rooms were lit but he could see no sign of their occupants. He was going to have to get closer. He cursed the bright moonlight. It was going to make it difficult for him. As he stood studying the ground, he saw a french door open and Kaddir's niece, Reba, stepped onto the verandah. Fletcher froze behind a bush. The girl closed the door behind her and walked over to the opposite corner of the verandah where a light shone from two small windows. Fletcher saw her stand close to the windows, as if listening to what was being discussed inside the room. Suddenly she abruptly turned and hurriedly retraced her steps. As she disappeared back inside the bungalow a man appeared from around the corner of the building. It was the man Fletcher had seen with the girl at Ali's club. The man looked thoughtfully at the french doors, and then followed the girl's example and entered the bungalow.

Fletcher mentally sighed. It was going to be more difficult than he had expected. He decided to give the verandah a miss and try the rear of the building. He worked his way along the driveway until he came to the car. It was a taxi with a local registration number. He made a mental note of its number and glanced inside. Lying on the rear seat was a suitcase. His pulse quickened. On the side of the suitcase was a hotel label, and it looked like one of the Grand Hotel! He quickly knelt down, out of view from anyone inside the bungalow. The suitcase also had a name label attached to it! The name of the person who was inside the bungalow with Kaddir. He glanced up at the car. If he opened one of the car doors it would illuminate the inside and attract attention. He saw that the driver's window was open, but it was on the far side. For several seconds he remained where he was and then inched his way around the front of the car to the open window. Fortunately it was out of view of the verandah. He withdrew a small pocket torch and leant inside the car. The beam from the torch shone on the label and he read the name – J.A. Wilson! My God, he thought, Wilson! Could it be the same one? His torch picked out the hotel label. It was the Grand Hotel! It could only be the same Wilson, he thought, and admired the level at which they operated. There was no need for him to go near the bungalow. He could check at the airport and then contact Spencer. But as the thoughts entered his mind, he also had an immediate feeling of danger. He quickly turned away from the car, but he was not quick enough! A hard instrument smacked into the side of his head sending him reeling to the ground. A blinding pain made him helpless and a vicious blow to his stomach made him retch and gasp for air.

He felt himself being lifted under the armpits and dragged across the driveway, but he was incapable of resisting. His head throbbed and yellow lights danced in front of his eyes. He was only half conscious of being dragged along a corridor and into a brightly-lit room. He heard voices, but couldn't identify the words. The pressure under his arms was suddenly released and he felt himself sitting in a chair. He tried to clear his head, but the pain still screeched at him.

'Well, well, Fettos,' a voice said. It had an unfamiliar ring about it.

Fletcher forced himself to look at the voice. He could bear the pain now, only just, but he could keep it under control. A hazy figure danced in front of him, but it gradually stood still. It was Kaddir. He stood a few feet away, a sardonic smile on his face.

'How very considerate of you to come to us,' Kaddir said again.

Fletcher ignored him and looked for Wilson. He found him standing close to Kaddir, but Wilson didn't appear as pleased as Kaddir.

'Hullo, Wilson,' Fletcher mumbled, and was thankful he was able to speak.

'You know this man?' Kaddir asked sharply.

'He has been staying at my hotel,' Wilson replied in his customary accent. 'A journalist.'

'Journalist!' Kaddir scoffed. 'This man is a British agent.'

'A British agent!' Wilson retorted. There was a note of concern in his voice.

'Yes,' Kaddir sneered. He appeared to be enjoying the situation. 'In fact,' he added, 'we have already tried to dispose of him.'

'I trust you will now succeed,' Wilson said anxiously.

'Have no fear,' Kaddir replied. 'We will deal with him.'

Fletcher braced himself.

'Just for the record, Wilson,' he said. 'The man you are selling arms to is a Russian agent.'

Kaddir laughed. Wilson didn't appear to be troubled.

'If we can finalize our details,' Wilson said

to Kaddir.

'Certainly,' Kaddir replied. 'You have a plane to catch.' He spoke sharply in a strange tongue. Fletcher mustered every available ounce of energy. His life was at stake. He tried to stand upright but his legs wouldn't hold him. He felt himself falling and a hammer-like blow crashed into his face. Everything went black...

Eventually his unconsciousness gave way to a pitch blackness, and then a grey fog of mental confusion as his brain started to register. Two dazzling lights seemed to bore into him. He put out his hand to grab the lights and felt himself falling ... falling... It was dark again and there was nothing to grab onto. He had to stop himself from falling... He moved his arms, but they didn't respond! Desperately he struggled to move his arms, but they wouldn't move... And he was falling! Suddenly a whirlpool of lights flashed around him and he stopped falling. A figure loomed up in front of him and started to pommel his head and body with blows. He could feel each of the blows, but he was helpless to defend himself! His arms wouldn't move! The blows became more ferocious. He could feel himself screaming, but he heard nothing! Suddenly it was over... He was with people looking out to sea. Dark faces and white suits surrounded him. He could see them talking, but he heard nothing. There was no sound and the figures moved with a slow, awkward gait. Then again the whirlpool of coloured lights, again the man pommelling him with blows, and then the bottomless pit. Suddenly he was walking along a rough metal track, towards a small white building. He started to run, but the building still remained in the distance. He could feel panic grip his body. He had to reach the building. His movements seemed to get slower ... slower... He looked behind him and saw people running towards him. He had to get away from them. The vision of the white building vanished and he was engulfed by a green vapour ... and then darkness.

Chapter Six

Fletcher moved his body and stretched his arms. With his hands he felt the hard surface of timber boards under his body. He opened his eyes and saw the dark, uneven surface of the ceiling above him. Simultaneously, his head and stomach registered their protest. He closed his eyes. His head throbbed, pounded, and his stomach became twisted with pain. The pain subsided and he put his hand to his head and felt a bandage. Who had done that? he wondered. He ran his hand over his face and felt the stubble of a beard. He recalled being dragged into a room with Kaddir and Wilson, but it seemed a long time ago. How long had he been unconscious? Where was he now? He opened his eyes again and forced them to remain open. He saw the roof above him formed of stone slabs and roughly-hewn timbers. He dragged himself into a seated position and breathed heavily to stop his stomach from rebelling. He was in a room of about twelve feet square and the same height. It had bare stone walls and an earthen floor. Narrow openings where the room met the walls served both as a means of ventilation and for lighting purposes. There was a single, heavy wooden door, with no handle or furniture. He was lying on a wooden bunk. But where was he and how long had he been there? He looked at his clothing. His jacket had been taken from him. He was in his shirt and slacks, and they looked grubby as if he had been travelling steerage. Again he ran his hand over his stubble. It was a two-day growth, he thought. What had he been doing? His mouth felt parched with a sickly taste. He had been drugged, he thought. For two days he had been kept in a state of semi-consciousness by drugs. He moved his legs off the bunk and tried to stand up. His legs felt heavy and he ached in every limb. He sat down again. He had a vague impression of someone pommelling him with blows to the body, and realized it was not something he had imagined. But where had they brought him? The room was stifling hot. Was he still in Greece? He looked around the room and saw nothing which helped to tell him where he was. He glanced at the openings in the wall and saw only a clear blue sky. His stomach rebelled again and he lay back on his bunk. Why had Kaddir kept him alive? he wondered. Why had he not disposed of him as he had said to Wilson?

After a while the pain in his stomach subsided and he was able to stand up and walk about. At least he was alive, he thought, and one of Nico's men would have been watching the bungalow. Nico and Toni would know who to contact. But where was he? Where had they taken him?

He thought about Wilson who was flying to Baghdad to arrange a shipment of supplies for the American party. Was he also arranging a supply of arms for Kaddir from the same place? And was Kaddir a Kurd? Had Timovsky been trying to utter his name, or had he been trying to warn him about the Kurds? And what about the American party? Had he any real grounds for his suspicions? There was a leak somewhere. Could it be one of them? Were any of them in a position to get access to classified information? What was there about Young and Marlow which gave the C.I.A. cause for concern?

Suddenly he heard a bolt on the outside of the door being withdrawn. He stopped in his tracks and waited. Another bolt was withdrawn and the lock turned. He held his breath. The door opened and his heart sank, Two men were standing in the doorway. Two dark, swarthy tribesmen! They were dressed in a strange garb – a mixture between the dress of a Turkish peasant and an Afghan tribesman. Over their rough, flannel-type shirts, they wore colourful waistcoats. Their trousers were pantaloons tucked into a pair of black leather riding boots. On their heads they wore Persian-type headscarfs.

One of the men said something in

Kermanji and stood to one side. Cautiously Fletcher crossed over to the doorway. It opened onto a tiled verandah. Along one side was a stone, dwarf wall, with a number of piers supporting the roof. It was like the prison block of an army barracks. As he stepped onto the verandah he could see a cluster of small, squat, white buildings. But it was the view beyond, that made him realize how desperate was his position. Rising steeply behind the building was a backcloth of pale green and yellow. Above that, the rugged face of a mountain towered into the sky! As he moved further along the verandah he could see the mountains all around him, and they had an unfamiliar look about them. He was not still in Greece as he had secretly hoped. He was somewhere deep in the heart of Kurdistan!

They descended a short flight of steps on to an open square of earth, baked hard by the fierce sun. The white buildings of a settlement surrounded the square. The men roughly gripped his arms and led him towards one of the larger buildings which looked like a meeting house. Fletcher looked around for signs of life, and saw only four horses tethered to a rail. He glanced up at the sun. It was at its highest peak. It was midday, the time when most people in the East were indoors.

They reached the entrance to the building

and one of the Kurds opened the door and pushed Fletcher through the opening. He found himself in a long, narrow room, like an assembly hall. He heard the door being closed behind him and walked further into the room. It had a wooden floor and white-washed walls, with narrow, slit windows, at roof level. At the opposite end were two curtained openings. The only furniture in the room was at the far end, where three cushions lay on the floor around a short-legged table. As Fletcher stood taking stock of his surroundings, two men entered the room. One was Kaddir, the other a much older, and more robust man, with a rugged, weather-beaten face. They were both dressed in the same type of costume as the Kurds who had brought him from the cell, but Kaddir's costume was more colourful, and his waistcoat was edged with silver trimmings.

Kaddir and his companion sat, squat-legged, at the table.

'Come, Mr Fettos,' Kaddir said in English, and indicated the cushion opposite him.

Fletcher walked over to them, his eyes on the older man. His face had a familiar ring about it. As he got closer to the men, he recognized him. It was Serif Kahn, one of the leaders of the Kushgai tribe who had fled from the Persians after the abortive uprising in 1946. There was no question about it. His

135

features had changed with the passing of years, but Fletcher could still see the resemblance to the photograph he had looked at in Peekas' office. So Kaddir was Kahn's son after all, he thought, and wished he had voiced his suspicions to Spencer. He took his place on the cushion opposite Kaddir and the old man. Kaddir had a satisfied smile on his face, but the older Kurd looked stern and unfriendly.

'How do you feel?' Kaddir asked, again in English.

'Lousy,' Fletcher growled. 'I could do with a drink.'

'It will come,' Kaddir smiled. 'We are not inhospitable. It is a pity you are still suffering from the after-effects of the drugs, but you were rather difficult to handle and required more than the customary dose.'

'Good,' Fletcher retorted. 'I wouldn't like you to think that I am pleased to be here, wherever we are.'

'You are at my training camp,' Kaddir said. 'In the mountains.'

'Turkey, Iraq or Persia?' Fletcher asked.

'Turkey,' Kaddir beamed. 'But don't worry, Fettos, you are not far from civilization. Kiran is only about forty kilometres away. That is if you know the passes through the mountains. We even get visitors to our camp. Americans!' He laughed openly as he referred to the Americans.

136

'Americans?' Fletcher asked ignoring his amusement.

'Yes, Americans,' Kaddir replied. 'They come here about twice a year and bring us medical supplies. They look at our crops, our cattle, and our children.' He chuckled. 'They do not know that we get our own supplies and doctors from our friends.'

'The Russians,' Fletcher added.

Kaddir bowed his head. 'As you say, Fettos, the Russians.'

The curtains behind Kaddir were pulled to one side, and one of the men who had escorted Fletcher to the hall entered with a tray, which he placed on the table and quickly departed. From a goatskin jug Kaddir poured a pale, milky-looking liquid, into three mugs. He handed one to Fletcher and the other to the old man who was obviously unable to understand what they were talking about.

Fletcher purposely waited until one of the Kurds took a drink before satisfying his thirst. It was a form of yoghurt, a stable diet of the Kurds, but not a very pleasant drink to anyone who had not acquired the taste. However, Fletcher gladly drank the rancid goats milk. Kaddir then offered him a piece of wafer-thin bread, another everyday food of the tribespeople.

'Why have you brought me here?' Fletcher asked.

'As a safeguard,' Kaddir said.

'Safeguard?' Fletcher asked. 'Against what?'

'Against the non-delivery of certain supplies,' Kaddir beamed.

Fletcher looked puzzled.

'You see the man who is arranging the shipment is of your race,' Kaddir said quietly, 'and he was most perturbed when he learned who you were working for. So long as you are alive I feel certain we shall get our supplies. Otherwise we might let you loose and his position would be in great jeopardy.' He gave a supercilious smile. 'It appears our friend has a high regard for his position in your society.'

Fletcher felt a fleeting moment of gratitude for Wilson. But for him he would not be alive.

'And after the delivery of your shipment?' he asked.

Kaddir made a resigned gesture.

'There are certain people who would like to question you,' he said.

Fletcher knew who.

'Some of my men will take you to them. After that...' He threw up his hands and smiled.

Fletcher gritted his teeth. If they ever got him over the border into the Soviet Union, he was in for a rough time.

'It is regrettable,' Kaddir said. 'You are a

very worthy adversary.'

'Adversary?' Fletcher asked. 'Why? Why should we be opposed? I have no fight with you?'

He knew the answer, but he wanted Kaddir to spell it out for him.

'We are opposed,' Kaddir replied. 'We are, Fettos. You work for the British.'

'And you the Russians.'

'Let us say that a Communist type of regime would be more suitable for my brothers who live in these mountains.'

Fletcher wondered whether this was the old man's belief as well, but didn't ask, it wasn't necessary. Kaddir answered for him, as if he had read his thoughts.

'Oh! my father does not know of this yet. He is an old man and has the dreams of an old man. But his days are finished. He will be told in due course, and so will our kins people.'

'And the present discussions being carried out with the Turkish Government?' Fletcher asked.

'Talk, talk, talk!' Kaddir sneered. 'I want no part of that and I told them so. The only things that will make the Turkish Government take notice are bullets.' His eyes became ablaze. 'What about the promises made to our people during your war with the Turks? What about the treaties of Sèvres and Lausanne. What about them? What happened to Sheik Said and Dr Fuad?'

He was quoting from history. A history of broken promises which had led to the rebellion of 1925, when the Turks had brutally put down a Kurdish attempt to set up an independent Kurdistan. But Fletcher knew that Kaddir wasn't interested in the negotiations because it would bring a settlement to their differences and that wouldn't suit the Russians. Kaddir was going to have to make his move very soon, otherwise he would not be able to rally support.

'When my father and I fled from our lands in Persia,' Kaddir continued, 'we came to live in this valley. I vowed then that one day I would continue the battle. That is why I came back.'

'Back?' Fletcher asked. 'From the Soviet Union?'

'Yes,' Kaddir replied. 'From the Soviet Union. You see, Fettos, I went there to make preparations for our next attempt to establish our independence, and I have been well trained.'

Very well, Fletcher thought. The Russians were being presented with an ideal person to mould into their pattern. A man who the tribespeople would accept as their leader, by birth, and a man who was eager to throw down the gauntlet to the Turks.

'So this is where you have trained your men to work for Russian Intelligence.'

140

'They have been working for me,' Kaddir said, emphasizing his authority, 'and one or two aids from the Soviets. We have selected our men very carefully and trained them thoroughly. This is a well-equipped camp, Fettos. We have all the necessary aids. They are prepared for any task.'

'More assassinations?' Fletcher asked.

'If necessary,' Kaddir replied without hesitation. 'If necessary we will kill all of those who have leanings to the West.'

'That might be an impossible task.'

'No, my friend, not impossible. You see these people react differently to your race. Already there are signs that many notable people who have Western sympathies are changing their views. They are beginning to question the strength of your intelligence, but most of all, they are beginning to fear for their safety.'

Fletcher felt a sudden feeling of helplessness. Here was Kaddir admitting to being the master mind behind a diabolical scheme to assassinate all people of prominence who showed Western tendencies, just as Spencer had predicted, and Fletcher could do nothing about it. He was too weak from his ordeal to attempt to kill the wily Kurd, and the possibility of escape seemed remote. But whilst Kaddir was in a confidential mood, he decided to play on it.

'And what do the Soviets give you in

return? Weapons?'

'No, not weapons,' said Kaddir. 'They are too clever to become so directly involved. No, they will give us their support the moment we make our move. They will make their voices heard in the chambers of the United Nations, and they will give their warning to Turkey. These mountains belong to us, Fettos. Not the Turks, Persians or Syrians, but to us.'

'Nor the Russians.'

'No, not even the Russians, but if the Turkish army moves in again like they did in 1925, we may ask the "bear" to come to our aid.' He leant forward, 'And they will come.'

Perhaps, Fletcher thought, perhaps. They were itching to get control of the mountains, but whether they would risk a direct confrontation with Turkey was another matter. But whatever happened, Turkey was going to be placed in an invidious position. The reasons for Breznov's visit to Baghdad and Cairo were apparent. Besides laying the necessary plans for Kaddir to start his uprising, he was also getting diplomatic support for when the Russians made their stand in support of the Kurds. Fletcher was also beginning to understand why Kaddir had gone in search of weapons. The Russians liked to make grandiose schemes in the safety of their Kremlin, they didn't like to get their fingers burned. They could have

of his limbs.

He had sat in this position for what felt like an eternity when a faint scratching noise made him sit up sharply. Instantly his reflexes were alert. Again he heard the noise. His pulse quickened. The bolt was being carefully withdrawn! He wasn't mistaken. Again he heard the bolt being moved! Then he heard the lock being turned. He braced himself and mustered every available ounce of energy. When the door opened he would make a break for it, even if it meant doing battle with the guard. The lock lever clicked back into its casing, but before the door opened, a voice whispered, 'Come!' in English.

Fletcher remained silent. Who was it? What was happening? He waited. Again the voice whispered, 'Come!'

Fletcher hesitated. It could be a trap. Once outside the door he could find a rifle barrel waiting to blast him into kingdom come. On the other hand it might be a means of escape! He had to take the risk. With heart thumping he slipped out of the doorway.

It was dark outside, but not as dark as in the cell, and a half moon gave a dim light. Fletcher looked straight into the dark, unfamiliar face of a Kurd. The Kurd moved aside to let him past. Fletcher stepped on to the verandah and saw his two guards propped up against the wall, nearby. They looked as if they had been drugged – or killed! He didn't bother to find out. Swiftly he crept away from the doorway and into the dark corner of a nearby building. He watched the Kurd relock the door. Who was he? What was he up to?

The Kurd came up to him, tugged at his sleeve, and crept away. Cautiously Fletcher followed, watching the shadows. The Kurd darted into the shadow of another building. Fletcher hesitated, and then followed him. When he caught up with him, the man started to move off. Fletcher grabbed him and held him back.

'Where are we going?' Fletcher asked in Turkish.

The Kurd tried to get out of his grip, but Fletcher held him. He repeated the question in Arabic.

'Come,' the Kurd whispered in English. 'Friend, come.'

'Who sent you?' Fletcher hissed in Turkish.

'Friend, come.'

They were the only words he appeared to know.

Fletcher looked into his rough, scarred face. He was going to get nothing out of him, and they couldn't afford to stand there arguing. He had to trust him, but he didn't like it. It was all too easy.

He let the man go, and watched him skirt the buildings and take a narrow track which led down the slope. Fletcher took one last look around him and then followed in the Kurd's path.

Chapter Seven

Stealthily Fletcher followed the Kurd into the valley. Behind him, the squat buildings of the settlement were silhouetted in the moonlight against the towering mountains. Across the valley came the glow from a number of camp-fires.

They passed through a terraced garden of crops and came to a copse. The Kurd signalled Fletcher to remain where he was, whilst he went ahead. Fletcher watched him disappear into the wood and waited tensely, the cold night chilling his body.

Presently, he saw a slim, dark figure, come out of the copse leading two ponies. He went forward to meet them, but it wasn't until he was upon them that he saw the face of the person who had arranged his escape. It was Kaddir's niece, Reba! The girl he had helped at the meeting in Cairo University. The Kurd was nowhere about. He had vanished into the valley.

'You!' Fletcher exclaimed. 'Why?'

'We must be quick,' she whispered in English, ignoring his question. 'Put this on.'

She handed him a thick woollen sweater.

'Why?' he insisted, pulling the jumper over

151

his jacket.

'Oh! there isn't time for questions,' she pleaded. 'You must trust me.'

Fletcher let the matter drop. He had no option, but to trust her. She pulled one of the ponies towards him and held it while he mounted. He made himself comfortable on the saddle. It was a small, sturdy beast. Reba got hold of a leading rein, fastened to the bridle of Fletcher's pony, and lithely got into the saddle of her beast. She swung her pony towards the copse and gave it a gentle kick. Slowly they moved forward. Fletcher glanced back at the settlement. It was still peaceful.

They followed a narrow track through the trees until they came to the bed of the valley, where they headed west towards the dark mass of mountains. They travelled in silence, and the only sounds that could be heard were the barking of a dog and the cry from a stray sheep. After a while they started to climb. At first it was a gradual rise, but later it became more severe. Fletcher held the reins with one hand and steadied himself with the other, as his mount negotiated the uneven ground. Several times the horses' feet disturbed loose rocks which rolled noisily away from them into the valley. Fletcher hung on doggedly as the going became more difficult. He had no conception of what was on either side of him. He could feel the air getting cooler and occasionally caught a glimpse of a campfire far below him.

Eventually the climb became less severe, but a strong wind met them head on. Reba urged her pony forward. A sheer rock face loomed up at them on their right side, whilst to the left was the inky blackness of a deep gorge. Once or twice Fletcher's pony stumbled and it took all his strength to keep on the saddle. They inched their way through the pass and started to descend, but the descent became even more difficult to negotiate than the climb. Fletcher was thrown about in his saddle and could feel his energy sapping. He brought out all his reserves of willpower and hung on doggedly. They came to the bottom of the valley and forded a stream, but Reba didn't call a halt. Nor did she make any move to engage him in conversation. Relentlessly she urged her pony forward, past a cascading waterfall and into another pass.

For Fletcher the nightmare ride seemed never ending. From valley to pass and into valley. Climbing, descending. Rocks, screes, rivers, followed one after another. The darkness stated to give way to the cold grey light of dawn and still they carried on. Stoically Fletcher endured his torture. He had long since stopped thinking about Kaddir, or any other matter which had previously occupied his thoughts. The lean figure of Reba bounced in front of his eyes until he could see it no more. Even when she stopped and dismounted he still remained rooted to his saddle. She pulled at his arm and he slid off his pony onto the ground. He struggled to his feet and dimly watched her lead the ponies to a stream. He saw a nearby tree and crawled under its branches. As his head touched the ground he fell into a deep sleep.

When Fletcher awoke, he felt the heat of the sun on his body. For a while he lay quite still. His brain recalled the ride and his limbs simultaneously made their resentment felt. He ached in every joint, and his stomach reminded him that it had forgotten when it had last been replenished.

He opened his eyes and saw the green leaves of the tree all around him, giving a measure of protection from the fiery ball which hung directly overhead. He raised himself up on his elbow and saw the steep rock faces of the mountains on either side of the narrow valley. The floor of the valley was a baked dry river bed, but in the centre of the yellow clay was the trickle of a stream. The sight of it made him feel better. But where was Reba? Without her he was lost! He sat upright and gave a sigh of relief when he saw the two ponies standing quite still in the shade of a nearby tree. Then he saw Reba coming from the stream. He relaxed and watched her walk towards him. She had discarded the thick woollen clothing she had been wearing during the night. She was dressed in a pair of light khaki trousers and open-necked shirt. Her hair was fastened with a ribbon at the back of her head and her round, tanned face looked more beautiful to Fletcher than he had seen before.

She came up to him, a smile on her face.

'Feel better?' she asked.

'Much,' Fletcher agreed.

He noticed his pullover lying close by. Reba must have removed it whilst he slept. She handed him a goatskin water jug, and Fletcher slowly satisfied his thirst. She went to the saddle of her pony and returned with some food.

'Do all the people in these mountains eat nothing but bread?' Fletcher asked jokingly.

'On special occasions they might slaughter a sheep,' she smiled.

'I hope I'll be invited one day,' he said, but the bread tasted good and it helped to fill the gap.

She sat down beside him.

'Where are we?' he asked.

'About twenty kilometres from Kiran,' she replied.

Only twenty from Kiran, he thought. Kiran and Maxwell! He felt much better. He was in striking distance of foiling Kaddir. But they weren't out of the woods yet. Kaddir would send some of his men after them. He said so to Reba.

'Yes,' she replied thoughtfully, 'he will, but we are off the recognized route, and if we keep under cover during the day we will be able to get to Kiran this evening.'

Fletcher looked around him. They were well camouflaged by the tree, so were the horses.

'But they will be looking for you in Kiran. You will have to take care.'

Fletcher grunted. Once he had passed on the information to Maxwell, he could look after himself.

'Why have you done this?' he asked. He was genuinely puzzled.

'It is my grandfather's wish that you escape,' she said quietly.

'Serif Kahn?' Fletcher asked.

'Yes,' she said. 'He is my grandfather. Kaddir is my uncle.'

'Why does Serif Kahn wish this?'

Reba sighed.

'My grandfather has always been suspicious of the Russians. He fears them more than the Turks or Persians, and he knows now that my uncle is working for them.'

'I see,' said Fletcher. He more or less had the picture now, but he didn't see where Reba fitted into it.

'What about your parents?' he asked.

'My father was Kaddir's brother,' she explained. 'He was killed in the fighting with the Persians shortly before I was born.

When our tribe fled into Turkey they came and lived in the valley where you were taken to. However, my mother married again, to a man from another tribe and we went to live in another settlement, further South. I was brought up with them, but as I was Serif Kahn's only grandchild I spent a lot of time with him.'

'And what about Kaddir?'

'He remained in the settlement with my grandfather. My grandfather never gave up his dream of uniting all the people of the mountains and forming a country of our own. He was never allowed to by my uncle. About six years ago my uncle left the settlement and went to the Soviet Union. This was against my grandfather's wishes. He came back, last year, and since then everything has changed.'

'How?' Fletcher asked.

'Oh! my uncle had many meetings with the leaders of the tribes. He tried to get them to agree to fight the Turks.'

'And did they?'

'No. Most of them would not hear of it and urged peaceful negotiations. My uncle was furious and would have nothing more to do with them. He started collecting men together who would support him and trained them in the settlement. Those in the settlement who were against him were forced to leave.'

157

'Did your grandfather support him?'

Reba looked sad. 'He is an old man and my uncle was able to persuade him that it was only a safeguard in case the Turkish Government wasn't prepared to negotiate and sent their army to occupy the valleys. But about six months ago two men came to the settlement from the Soviet Union and my grandfather began to suspect that my uncle was working for them and not our people. The two men remained for a week. When they left, a number of my uncle's men went with them.'

'To be sent abroad to act as Soviet agents,' Fletcher said.

'So it would seem,' Reba said. 'The man who started the trouble at Cairo University was one of them.'

'Why did Kaddir take you with him to Cairo and Athens?' Fletcher asked.

'My grandfather told him to. My uncle said he was going to meet a number of influential people who would help their cause. He could not refuse my grandfather's request without arousing his suspicions.'

'Who did he meet in Cairo?' Fletcher asked hopefully.

'I do not know,' Reba replied. 'He often went out alone. The only person I saw him talking to was the man who came to our villa in Piraeus.'

'Wilson,' Fletcher explained. 'He came to

arrange a shipment of arms.'

'I cannot understand why,' Reba said. 'He has many weapons.'

It puzzled Fletcher also.

'Do you know when the shipment is due to arrive?' he asked.

Reba shook her head.

'No,' she said, 'but I think it must be very soon.'

So did Fletcher.

'I did overhear my uncle talking to one of his men and Zamdi was mentioned.'

'Zamdi!' Fletcher said thoughtfully. 'Where is that?'

'On the border with Iraq. About thirty kilometres from Kiran.'

Close enough to stop any shipment, Fletcher thought, and felt a little easier.

'What did your uncle tell your grandfather about me?' he asked.

'He said you were a British agent who was spying for the Turkish Government, and that you should be kept a prisoner until the outcome of the negotiations.'

'Your grandfather believed him?'

'My grandfather asked Kaddir to bring you to him. My grandfather does not understand English so Kaddir obeyed him. However, my grandfather got me to hide in a room behind the curtains and I overheard what was said. When my grandfather learned that Kaddir was working for the Russians he was very sad, and arranged for your escape.'

'What will happen to him?' Fletcher asked.

Reba looked dejected. 'He knew the risk,' she said, 'and he is Kaddir's father.'

'What about you?'

'I am only obeying my grandfather,' she said quietly, 'but I also want to stop my uncle. For centuries our people have been involved in wars and fighting. They have been massacred by the Turks and the Persians. Why should there be more bloodshed, when we can settle our differences peacefully?'

Why indeed, Fletcher thought, but he knew the answer. Because it suited the Russians' aims at getting control of the mountains and the personal ambitions of one man – Kaddir. But who was giving Kaddir his orders, he wondered. Was it one of the American party?

'Why did you go to the meeting at the University?' he asked.

'To hear the talk,' she replied, 'but I did not expect any trouble.'

'Did your uncle know?'

'No, he thought I was sightseeing.'

'Had you seen any of the party who were on the stage before?'

'Yes, all of them. They have all visited my step-father's settlement. They bring medicine and books. They do a lot of good work.'

'All of them? Are you certain?'

'Yes,' she said, puzzled by his question. 'I am sure.'

That would include Lipman, Fletcher thought. The one man he was not too sure about.

'The woman?' he asked. He didn't rule her out, neither.

'Yes, many times. She more than the rest.'

'Would they have visited your uncle's camp?'

'Yes, I know the Americans visited my uncle, but I do not know who was in the party.'

'Your grandfather said he approached some Westerners to ask their Government for support to his claim for an independent Kurdistan. Could that have been to one of them?'

'There have been no other Western visitors?' she replied.

No other Western visitors, Fletcher thought. So in the past twelve months a party of American workers had visited Kaddir's camp. They had been asked to pass on a message to Washington, which they had not done. The field was narrowing.

He was about to question her further, when she abruptly turned and held up her hand for him to remain silent. She crept away from him and stood beside the ponies under the trees. In the distance Fletcher watched six horsemen descend from the pass into the valley – six armed Kurds. He moved further into the confines of the tree as

the horsemen crossed the stream and followed the trail which brought them within
fifty yards of their position. He glanced up at
the sun and was glad it was behind them. He
also saw the buttocks of their two ponies
sticking out from the shade of the tree.

The horsemen moved slowly, as if their
mounts were tired, and one of the rider's
head was slumped forward, as if asleep on
his horse. They came to the closest point
and passed by, but neither Fletcher nor
Reba made any move until they were almost
out of sight.

Reba came back to him.

'We must keep watch in case there are
more,' she said.

Fletcher agreed. He was impatient to get
to Kiran and Maxwell, but he couldn't take
the risk of being seen by any of Kaddir's
men.

Reba sat down beside him. He noticed her
eyes were red-rimmed from the lack of sleep
and he felt guilty. In his eagerness to question her about Kaddir, he had overlooked
the fact that she had been keeping watch
whilst he had slept. There were still a lot of
questions he wanted to ask, but he decided
they could wait.

'You get some sleep,' he said. 'I'm all right
now.'

She gave a faint smile and curled up close
to him. Soon she was sleeping peacefully.

Fletcher replenished the water jug from the stream and returned to their hidden position. For a while he admired the beauty of the valley. The mountains along both sides towered towards the sky their peaks hidden from his view, but in the distance he could see other snow-capped peaks glistening in the sun. It was not the first time he had visited this range of mountains, but on previous occasions he had been further North and accompanied by a Turkish guide. The area, in which he now found himself, was a vast area of rugged terrain. An unmapped, mountainous region, in which only the sturdy survived. A number of tribes had settled in the more fertile valleys and cultivated their crops, but many others preferred to live off their flocks of sheep and goats, and moved from valley to valley according to the season. The Turks had done little to help them, and the unyielding nature of the country gave the Turks little encouragement to develop its resources. But it was a formidable barrier between Turkey and the Soviet Union, and for that reason alone the Turks would not hand over its sovereignty to the tribespeople. Even if Kaddir succeeded in starting a flame and uniting the tribes to a common cause, it would take a strong measure of support from other countries to make the Turks change their attitude. But Fletcher knew only too well that internal trouble was what the Communists thrived upon. He had little doubt that they had not already prepared the way for support of the Kurdish cause amongst the many unaligned nations, as well as with their own bloc. And if it caught the West off guard, it would put them in a stronger position.

Reba awoke from her sleep during the afternoon. There had been no further sign of any horsemen in the valley, but there was no telling who might be hidden away in the mountains, so they remained hidden by the tree.

Fletcher questioned her further, hoping for some clue which would indicate if Kaddir had any link with any other agents. But if Kaddir was being given orders from other sources, he had kept the fact from Reba. On the question of arms, however, Reba was more informative. Kaddir had received previous shipments of arms, mainly rifles and sub-machineguns, and from her description of the weapons it appeared they were of British manufacture. It was also apparent that they had not been supplied from the International Syndicate, but from Arab sources, smuggled through the mountains from Syria and Iraq. Again Fletcher wondered why Kaddir had finally had to look elsewhere.

As they sat and talked, Fletcher couldn't help but ponder on the unusual circumstances in which he now found himself. He had suddenly been moved hundreds of miles from his normal centre of operations to a mountainous gorge, and into the company of a beautiful Kurdish woman. It was an occupation not for the faint in heart. But Reba's presence helped to make it all worth while. She talked freely about her youth and the simple life they lived on their settlement. She had not travelled far, and only on three occasions had she ever left the mountains, the last one being with Kaddir. She had been taught to speak English by her teacher, and the Americans whom she had met in Kiran, where she had spent a lot of her time living with a relative.

But their talk was not only about Reba and the questions were not all from Fletcher. She in turn questioned him, and he found himself readily answering her. For a short while the reason for their being together was forgotten. But as soon as it turned dark Fletcher became impatient to be on their way.

They ate the last of their food and mounted their horses. Again Reba took the lead, but the going this time was much easier. The ground was hard and flat, and they made good progress. After about two hours, they came to another valley which cut across their route, running North and South. It was a much broader valley with a rough metal road which linked Kiran with the border town of Zamdi. They were back in civilization.

They kept close to the banks of the river which meandered its way through the valley, for fear of being silhouetted in the headlamps of a passing vehicle, but in their three-hour trek only one poorly-lit truck struggled along the road. They passed close to a number of small encampments and the bleating from stray sheep became an endless cry. Long before they reached Kiran they could see the lights of the town. A myriad of yellow dots spotted the darkness and a full glow hung over the town like a veil. The mountain slopes were also pin-pointed with the red glow from the fires of the tribal encampments.

When the town lay only a short distance ahead, Reba stopped and dismounted. Fletcher followed suit.

'It is better that you go on foot from here,' she explained. 'That is the Americans' camp.' She pointed to an area close to the river where Fletcher could see several rows of lights. 'You can't mistake it. They have a lot of huts.'

'And Zarb the cobbler?' Fletcher asked.

'If you follow the road, it will take you into the main square. In the corner of the square you will see a white-faced building. That is the Army Commandant's office. A narrow lane runs from alongside that building down to the river. You will find Zarb's shop about fifty metres along the lane. His name is above the entrance door.'

166

Fletcher memorized the instructions.

'Will you be safe?' he asked tenderly.

'Yes,' she said. 'I will be with my cousin and her husband. They have a farm about two kilometres north of the town. My uncle would not harm me there. It is too close to the military.'

'What is their name?' Fletcher asked.

'Lazar,' she replied.

'If all goes well, it will not be for long,' he said encouragingly. Once he contacted Maxwell, he thought, they would be able to alert the army and stop Kaddir.

He handed her the reins of his pony.

'How can I ever repay you?' he asked.

'You helped me once before,' she replied gently, 'and you will be helping me again, and my people.'

'I will see that the authorities are given all the facts,' he said, 'so that it will not harm your cause.'

For a moment he stood beside her, a little uncertain as what to say.

'I hope we will meet again,' he said finally.

'We will,' she replied tenderly, 'if it is Allah's wish.'

On a sudden impulse he bent forward and kissed her tenderly on the cheek.

'Goodbye,' he said and slipped away into the darkness.

Stealthily Fletcher skirted the road until it entered the town. Despite the lateness of the hour many of the buildings showed lights behind their shutters, but there was no one abroad. Fletcher kept to the shadows and entered the town. It had a frontier air about it. The buildings were primitive in design and construction, and the earth road surface was littered with horse and sheep droppings, baked hard with the sun.

Fletcher entered the square and recognized the Commandant's office. It was the only building with any semblance of smartness. Again keeping to the shadows and careful not to disturb a number of horses tied to a rail, he circumvented the square, and entered the dark alleyway in which Reba had told him he would find the cobbler's house.

In the darkness the cobbler was not easy to locate, and it was only by feeling the name, carved in the stone head over the door, that he was able to assure himself that he was not at the wrong building.

In response to his muffled knock, the lock was turned and the door opened, fractionally.

'Who is it?' a gruff voice asked in Turkish.

'A friend,' Fletcher whispered in the man's own tongue. 'I am looking for an American. I was told you could put me in contact with him.'

'Who told you that?'

'He did before he left Athens, three days ago.'

'The American base is down by the river,'

the man said, 'you can't miss it.' He started to close the door. Fletcher stopped him.

'I don't want the base,' he whispered hurriedly. 'I want to speak to the man who buys and sells information. It is important. He will reward you well.'

The door opened, and a tall, bald, powerfully-built Turk stood in the entrance. He weighed Fletcher up, saw that he was alone, and beckoned him to enter. Fletcher stepped into the shop, and the door was locked behind him.

The Turk struck a match and lit an oil lamp. It gave off a deep yellow light, displaying the cobbler's bench and samples of his craft. The cobbler came over to him and silently studied Fletcher's features, as if comparing them with something he had been told.

'Wait here,' he said finally. 'Don't answer the door to anyone. I will be back.'

He extinguished the light, leaving the room in darkness again, and left by another door.

Fletcher inspected both doors. They were locked, preventing him from leaving. But Spencer's message from Maxwell was to contact the cobbler, so he had little fear of having walked into a trap. He made himself comfortable on a stool and waited.

About an hour later he heard the cobbler return. The door from which he had left was unlocked, and the big man entered the room, together with another person who stood in the entrance.

When the Turk lit the lamp Fletcher saw it was Maxwell, and gave a sigh of relief.

'Stephen!' Maxwell said. 'Thank God you're safe!'

He came up to Fletcher and shook his hand warmly.

'Spencer told me to watch out for you,' Maxwell said, 'but I had little hope.' He patted Fletcher on the back. 'Man, it's good to see you.'

'And you,' Fletcher said and felt a load had been lifted off his shoulders.

Maxwell lit a cigarette. It was a different looking Maxwell to what Fletcher had previously seen. His face looked tanned and covered with sandy dust, as if he had been riding hard, and his khaki slacks and shirt were similarly soiled. Only his short, stubbly grey hair was as before.

'Well, man, let's hear about it,' Maxwell said eagerly.

Fletcher glanced at the Turk who was standing at the door watching them.

'He's all right,' Maxwell said. 'Besides, he doesn't understand English.'

Fletcher gave Maxwell his story. He told him everything and was glad to get it off his chest. It was someone else's responsibility now.

'The immediate area is simmering,' Max-

170

well said when he had finished. 'You can feel it everywhere you go. It's like sitting on top of a barrel of gunpowder not knowing when the fuse is going to be lit. We've had reports coming in, constantly, in the past twenty-four hours, of small tribal movements.'

He brought out a map from his hip pocket and spread it over the bench.

'All the movements seem to be towards this area,' he said, indicating a location about thirty miles south-east of their present position. It would be close to where Kaddir had his settlement, Fletcher thought, and said so.

'I thought as much,' Maxwell said, still looking at his map. 'In that case,' he added seriously, 'there are only two possible routes a supply train could get to that area.' He put his finger on the border post, Zamdi. 'There is a valley running East from here, about half a kilometre on the Iraqui side of the border. There is also another route from the same valley, about seven kilometres south.'

He indicated the second route. Both started in Iraq, but soon crossed the dotted line which indicated the Turkish border.

'There is a third route,' Fletcher added pensively.

Maxwell looked at him. 'The way you came out?' he asked.

'Yes,' Fletcher replied.

Maxwell shook his head.

'No,' he said, 'they wouldn't use that. If

171

they are getting a big shipment it will mean anything from a dozen to two dozen packed mules. Can you imagine them bringing them openly through the border control into Turkish territory?'

Fletcher couldn't.

'No,' Maxwell said firmly. 'They will use one of those two routes, and my guess is the one closest to Zamdi.' He looked at Fletcher. 'Well, it is up to the Turks now. We can only give them the facts.'

'What about the Iraqui Government? Won't they help?'

'Not with this one,' Maxwell said. 'My guess is that they will be involved up to their necks. Besides, it is not wise to show our hand too soon. If the Turks can get their traps laid up those valleys, they can stop them without any bother.'

'Let's hope there has been no change of plans.'

'We'll soon know. The Turks will put a 'plane up. It will spot any caravan heading for Zamdi.'

'What do you think Wilson is supplying? Ammunition?'

'Yes,' Maxwell replied firmly, 'Ammunition. When the Russians started to supply the Arab countries with their own weapons, the Arabs found themselves with a lot of surplus British arms.'

'Which they passed over to the Kurds.'

172

'Precisely. An ideal opportunity to arm the Kurds.'

'With British weapons.'

'But what they couldn't supply was the ammo' to go with the weapons. They hadn't any to give. So Kaddir has had to go into the international market. Once he gets his ammo' he is ready to make his move.'

Maxwell lit a cigarette and inhaled deeply. 'You had better keep out of sight for the time being in case Kaddir's men spot you. They will certainly be looking for you.' He turned and spoke to the Turk, asking him to fix Fletcher up with a bed and a meal. The Turk left the room.

'There is a room upstairs,' Maxwell explained. 'Not the Grand, but you will be safe. Zarb will fix you up with some food.'

'What are you going to do?'

'Get in touch with Colonel Sheriff as soon as possible. He is in Zamdi, but his sidekick, Major Ahmad, is here in Kiran. I've already primed them what to expect, and they are just itching to get hold of some evidence to move into the mountains. This shipment is just the excuse they are wanting.' He folded the map and placed it in his pocket. His face suddenly hardened. 'Anything else come to light?' he asked quietly.

'Maybe,' Fletcher said. 'According to Serif Kahn, he asked someone who visited the settlement to pass on a request to their Government to send a representative to talk with him about their move for independence. It would be interesting to know who he talked to.'

'Whoever it was, didn't pass it on,' Maxwell said grimly. 'That line of information is in my department. When do you say this was?'

'About nine months ago.'

Maxwell frowned. 'That lets out Lipman,' he said more to himself than to Fletcher.

'Lipman?' Fletcher asked.

'He worries me,' Maxwell grunted.

'And me,' Fletcher added.

'It shouldn't be too difficult to find out who went into that region, and when,' Maxwell said. 'They run their camp like a damned army establishment.'

'Who is here?' Fletcher asked.

'All of them, except Lipman and Dr Bradshaw. Lipman is in Baghdad, and Dr Bradshaw is arriving sometime tomorrow.'

Lipman wasn't the only one in Baghdad, Fletcher thought. Wilson was also there.

'Have you heard anything from Washington?' he asked.

Maxwell frowned. 'Yes,' he said. 'Marlow had been given a clearance.'

'What about Young?'

'They are still making enquiries.'

So Young still had a question mark over him, Fletcher thought, and with Marlow off the list there was no one else.

'Are you tired?' Maxwell asked.

'What did you have in mind?'

'A chat and a drink.'

'I'm not that tired,' Fletcher smiled.

'Good. I'll be back soon, but if anything goes wrong and I'm not back by dawn, contact Major Ahmad yourself. Tell him everything. He knows what to do.'

Maxwell slipped out of the shop, and the Turk took Fletcher to the room upstairs. It was sparsely furnished with a mattress, table, and two chairs. The Turk gave him some tough meat and black bread. Fletcher ate his fill and lay on the mattress. Was it really out of his hands now? he wondered. Was Kaddir now the responsibility of the Turks? And Lipman, Young, Marlow and Marsh the concern of Maxwell. Or were there further complications ahead?

It was a while before Maxwell returned. Fletcher was becoming anxious.

'What kept you?' Fletcher asked when the man entered the room.

'These,' Maxwell beamed, and placed a bottle of American Rye and two paper cups on to the table. From his hip pocket he produced a flask. 'Water,' he explained. 'I went back to the base.'

'And the Turks?' Fletcher asked.

Maxwell poured out two liberal measures from the bottle.

'Everything is under control,' he said. 'The

175

ball is in their court. Either they stop the shipment, or the balloon goes up.'

Fletcher allowed himself to relax.

'So we are finished?' he asked.

Maxwell handed him his cup. 'You are, perhaps,' he said, 'but not me. I'm going through to Zamdi in the morning to follow it up. There is a convoy of supplies for the base to collect, so I can kill two birds with one stone.'

'Supplies?' Fletcher asked. 'Is this the normal route?'

'It's not the best route, but it's the nearest to the base, and quickest. They fly them into Baghdad and Lipman ships them around. Medical and agricultural stuff, mainly. The convoy is due first thing, but the Turks won't let it through until they get a signature. I'll go through in the morning with a crew from the base. At the same time I can see what progress Colonel Sheriff is making. Care to come?'

'Sure,' Fletcher said eagerly. 'So long as I am no target for Kaddir.'

'We'll have to watch it,' Maxwell said seriously. 'We don't want any harm to come to you now. You've done your stuff.'

Maxwell sank his drink, poured another, and started to laugh to himself. He didn't explain his amusement and Fletcher didn't ask. He was also feeling elated.

'Man, we find ourselves in some funny

places,' Maxwell said suddenly, throwing out his arms. 'Look at this dump. Bare boards, stone walls, no ceiling, and a poky, filthy window, which hasn't been washed since it was first glazed. God! It's a hell of a life.' He recharged both cups. 'How did we ever get into this sordid business, Stephen?'

Fletcher gave a wry smile. It was a sordid business, he agreed. There was no code of rules. The only maxim which was accepted was that the ends justified the means. It was dog eat dog, and dangerous – highly dangerous. But he had known no other existence, it was part of him. There was no mystery about how he had got into it. He had been born into it! It was a family tradition. The British spy system existed on such traditions. Men devoted their life to its service. Men like Fletcher's father who had moved throughout the Balkans and Middle East, from Embassy to Embassy, Consulate to Consulate, and who had systematically trained and prepared his son to become part of the tradition. The die had been cast at birth, there had never been any alternative.

Fletcher looked wistfully into his cup as he thought of his parents and upbringing. They had been happy days.

He pulled himself up sharply and looked to see if Maxwell was waiting for him to give an answer. But Maxwell wasn't really interested in Fletcher's background, his thoughts were of his own.

'Thirty years ago,' Maxwell drawled, 'I was pounding the beat in a Chicago precinct. A nice steady sort of job. The hours weren't bad and the pay was reasonable.' He took a long drink and laughed. 'You know what?' he asked, 'I would have still been on that beat if the Station Sergeant hadn't encouraged me to study for my promotion exams. Yeah!' he laughed again. 'I would still be there. Probably would have got married and had kids.' He looked at Fletcher. 'You married?' Fletcher shook his head. 'No, it's not for us,' Maxwell grumbled. 'Study, the Sergeant said. Get on. Get off the beat. So I studied and look where it's got me.'

'A long way from Chicago,' Fletcher agreed.

Maxwell sighed heavily. 'Yeah! a long way. I suppose I can't blame the Sergeant. He meant well. How the hell was he to know there was going to be a war.'

So that was his background, Fletcher thought. From police work to Army Intelligence and then to the C.I.A.

'How long have you been out here?' Fletcher asked.

'Too damned long,' Maxwell grunted, and added less aggressively, 'Just under twenty years.'

Maxwell poured himself another drink. Fletcher watched him closely. There was something biting him, something on his mind. He had never seen Maxwell like this before.

'You know something?' Fletcher asked quietly, but seriously.

Maxwell turned to him, but just stared. Fletcher repeated the question. It got through to Maxwell.

'Maybe,' Maxwell frowned. 'I hope I'm damned well wrong.'

He had been back to the base for the liquor, Fletcher thought. He must have checked up on the trips into Kaddir's territory.

'Who?' Fletcher asked, but Maxwell wasn't telling.

'Too early,' he said. 'I should know more in the morning. I'll let you know then. I promise you.'

Fletcher let it drop. He could wait a further twenty-four hours.

The two men finished off the bottle and talked freely, but their discussions didn't return to either the nature of their work or to their present predicament. When Maxwell finally got up to leave, he was as sober as when he had arrived.

'There is a lane at the rear of the block,' he said to Fletcher before he left, 'which runs down to the river. Don't leave this room before ten-thirty, then go to the end of the lane. I will be waiting for you in a vehicle. O.K.?'

Fletcher nodded his head. 'Yes, ten-thirty it is.'

Maxwell gave a friendly smile.

'Let's hope tomorrow lives up to its expectations,' he said, and left the room.

Fletcher lay on the mattress, determined to analyse Maxwell's attitude, but fell into a deep sleep instead.

Chapter Eight

The following morning, Fletcher was awakened by the cobbler hammering on his last. The sunlight was streaming through the small window on to the bare boards. Fletcher got up from the mattress and looked out of the window. The narrow lane had become transformed into a busy shopping centre. Baskets of goods stood outside the narrow entrance doors to the shops, and a mixed crowd of Turkish peasants and Kurdish tribespeople went silently about their business. The Kurds were dressed in the flat cap attire imposed upon them by the Turks, not in the style Kaddir had favoured, but their womenfolk were wearing their colourful dresses. When one of them happened to glance in his direction, Fletcher quickly retreated from the window. He hadn't forgotten that Kaddir might be looking for him.

The hammering in the room below stopped, and a few minutes later the Turk entered the room, bringing a pot of coffee and some fresh fruit.

'It is ten o'clock,' he said.

Fletcher thanked him and asked if he

could have a bucket of water and the necessary kit to rid himself of his two-day growth. The Turk scowled, but returned soon after with the things Fletcher had requested. Quickly Fletcher got rid of his beard and ate his fill. When the Turk reappeared again and told him it was time to leave, Fletcher was physically, and mentally, prepared for anything.

From the small back room of the shop, used by the Turk as his living quarters, Fletcher came to the narrow lane which barely separated the two rows of dirty, yellow buildings. He cast a quick glance about him, saw that no one was watching, and ran and joined Maxwell who was sitting in a jeep, waiting for him. Maxwell greeted him with a silent wave and immediately drove off along the track which followed the river. When they left the town and joined the road for Zamdi, Maxwell became more communicative.

'This is some information I got from the exec. officer at the base,' he said, handing Fletcher two typed sheets. 'It lists the various expeditions which have taken place in the past twelve months, and the names of the people who went on them. I have marked the visits to Kaddir's settlement.'

Fletcher examined the sheets. There had been three visits to Kaddir's settlement. The first two had taken place close to each other, about nine months ago. About the time Serif

Kahn had made his request for help, Fletcher thought. The last visit had been recent. There were also other expeditions listed, but Fletcher didn't recognize the place names. He eagerly turned to the second sheet which listed the people who had taken part on the various expeditions. Each expedition had about twelve names alongside it. Marlow, Young and Carol Marsh had all been on the three expeditions to Kaddir's settlement. Lipman had also been on the last visit. But one name on the second and last visit to the settlement took Fletcher by surprise. It was Dr Bradshaw himself! Fletcher wondered. Bradshaw was a man of prominence. A man who could well be considered to have influence with his Government. A man to whom Serif Kahn could have well looked to for help.

'Dr Bradshaw,' he muttered.

'Yeah,' Maxwell grunted like a bear with a sore head. 'Dr Bradshaw!'

Fletcher handed the sheets back to Maxwell.

'What do you think?' he asked.

'He's a big fish,' Maxwell growled, 'and they are often overlooked.'

'Anything else on him?'

'Only that he was the one who laid on the second visit to Kaddir's settlement, and it was a quick follow up on the first.'

After he had read the reports of the first

expedition, Fletcher thought.

'And he went on the last visit,' Maxwell continued.

'So I see.'

Maxwell turned to him.

'Also, my friend, he is due to arrive at the base this evening.'

It was a chain of unfortunate coincidents, Fletcher thought.

'How is he placed in the Embassy?' he asked.

'Very highly,' Maxwell drawled and gripped the steering wheel. 'Hell, let's not jump to conclusions.'

No, Fletcher thought, let's not, but he knew Maxwell was. That's what had unsettled him the previous evening. He had got a whiff of the suspicions when he had been at the base to collect the liquor. That's what was making him now act like a bear with a sore head. Bradshaw was one of Maxwell's responsibilities, but he was so big that he had probably been left alone. Maxwell was going to have his work cut out.

'I see Lipman has been in the field,' Fletcher said changing the subject.

'They all have a spell in the field,' Maxwell replied. 'Lipman has been here several times.'

'You been with them?'

'Twice,' Maxwell said with a smile. 'Went out with Carol Marsh. On the last trip we got lost in the mountains and the Embassy cut up rough.'

'Pity you hadn't gone with Bradshaw?'

'Yeah,' Maxwell agreed ruefully.

'How long will it take us to get to Zamdi?'

'About three hours.'

'And then what?'

'See Colonel Sheriff, and bring the convoy back.'

'Anybody else meeting the convoy?'

'Yes. Young left earlier with some drivers.'

'Where are Marlow and Dr Marsh?'

'Marlow is visiting a new irrigation scheme, and Carol Marsh is at the base preparing to go into those mountains.' He waved his hand at the mountains to the East.

'A big practice,' Fletcher muttered more to himself.

'She works hard at it.'

Fletcher looked at the formidable barrier of mountains. If things didn't turn out as they hoped, she could well have more patients on her hands than she bargained for, he thought.

They drifted into silence. Maxwell sat gripping the steering wheel with a deep frown on his face. Fletcher turned his attentions to the mountain scenery and looked for a possible route into Kaddir's territory. He admired the cascading waterfalls, and studied the deep gorges which ran like stumpy fingers into the hillside. But the only accessible pass was the one through which he had travelled the previous evening with Reba. There was no other way except over the tops of the mountains.

He also kept a close watch on the small tribes that they passed, and had a few anxious moments when they were held up by sheep straying on to the track. Each delay made Maxwell more irritable and impatient, but Fletcher was concerned for his own safety. He was an easy target for any marksman hidden in the mountains, and he felt sure Kaddir would not let him off scot-free.

It was with a feeling of relief that they eventually saw Zamdi in the distance.

Maxwell stopped the jeep at the top of a hill, overlooking the post. A broad valley lay beneath them, with a group of buildings clustered around a bend in the river, and an old stone fort which towered over them. A blue haze hung over the buildings, and as far as the eye could see, small flocks of sheep were attacking the short, yellow grass, around tented encampments.

Maxwell handed Fletcher a pair of binoculars and indicated a group of huts adjacent to the fort.

'The army camp,' he said. 'The fort is only used as a stores depot.'

Fletcher picked out the camp and saw several armoured scout cars.

'A tough mob,' Maxwell muttered. 'Kaddir

will have his hands full with them.'

Fletcher turned his attention to the mountain range in the East. It towered into snow-packed peaks.

'Those scout cars will be no good in there,' he said.

'True,' Maxwell agreed, 'but Colonel Sheriff also has cavalry and foot soldiers in the valley ready to move in.' He pointed to a dark patch of mountains in the distance. 'That is one route into Kaddir's territory, the other is well out of view.'

'Where is the border?'

'On the far side of the town. You can see a row of vehicles waiting to pass through. Zamdi is in Turkish territory, but the valley to the South belongs to Iraq. So do the mountains to the West. Those to the East belong to Turkey.'

Fletcher picked out a row of army-type trucks, but the actual border post was hidden by a nearby building.

'Is there any other way Kaddir can get his supplies,' he asked.

Maxwell frowned. 'Only one,' he said, 'but it would take time.'

'How?'

'Smuggling them in in small doses. The Kurds operate a thriving business smuggling their produce into Iraq and Syria without much interference. Oh! the Turks know it is going on, but they turn a blind eye to it.

Occasionally they will make a search, but it is only to exercise their rights. All those tribes you can see in the valley move back and forward freely. What is to stop the supply train camping way down the valley and letting the supplies filter through slowly?'

'Only Kaddir's impatience,' Fletcher said.

'He has waited long enough. Another few months wouldn't do any harm.'

'What about the Russians?' Fletcher asked. 'They have to make their move soon, to restore their prestige with the Arab world. They don't want delays. Something could go wrong.'

'Perhaps,' Maxwell agreed. 'It was just a thought.' He replaced the binoculars in his case. 'We'll see what Colonel Sheriff has to say for himself.'

They drove into the valley, and the heat, dust, and smell of the small town, came up to greet them. It wasn't as big as Kiran, but it had a more eastern flavour about it. The narrow, single street, was an open bazaar with a mixed gathering of dark faces in varying garbs.

The army camp was set back from the town on the opposite side of the river. Maxwell drove up to the entrance and was stopped by a sentry. He showed his identity pass and was directed to the Colonel's office. Outside the block Maxwell looked thoughtfully at Fletcher.

'It might be as well if you remain here,' he said. 'There is no need to tell the Colonel all our secrets.'

Fletcher didn't argue. The less people who knew his occupation, the better. As Maxwell climbed the wooden steps up to the entrance to the building, Fletcher glanced casually at the office window. He saw the broad, white-jacketed back of a man move away from the window. He watched the window for a while, but the figure didn't reappear. He shrugged. He had thought the back had looked vaguely familiar.

He turned his attention to the border control point which was visible across the river. A wooden rail marked the border between Turkey and Iraq. On the Iraqui side were two wooden huts which housed their officials. It was a ridiculous-looking control, he thought. On both sides of the road, the sheep and goats freely crossed the imaginary line, and in the mountains, also, the Kurds moved without hindrance. It was only vehicles which were subject to controls.

The convoy of American trucks were parked in line ahead, on the Iraqui side of the border, waiting to cross into Turkey. There were eight vehicles, and on the Turkish side Fletcher saw a small group of khaki-clad civilians talking to the Turkish soldiers.

A tribe of Kurds moved slowly through the valley, the menfolk riding small, scraggy ponies, whilst the women, in their colourful dresses, walked dutifully behind, carrying bundles of clothing and utensils. Did they really want the independence that Kaddir was offering them? Fletcher wondered. Or were they, unwittingly, being made a tool of the Communists? He watched them pass into Iraq and recalled what Maxwell had said about smuggling the arms into Kaddir's territory. Perhaps, he thought, he had been too quick to refute the suggestion.

He was still thinking of this, and watching the tribe, when Maxwell rejoined him.

'There are two supply trains about thirty kilometres away,' Maxwell said eagerly, 'and there is another on its way. It looks as if they are going to try the Southern route.

'Tonight?' Fletcher asked.

'So the Colonel thinks. The trains have been camped for twenty-four hours resting the mules, so they will be fresh to move when it is dark.'

'What are the Turks going to do?'

'They have a company in the mountains already, keeping a watch on the train. When it is dark, tonight, they are moving two more in. As soon as the supply train steps into Turkish territory, they'll pounce.' Maxwell's face softened. 'We can do no more,' he sighed.

'Except wait,' Fletcher added.

'Not something I'm good at,' Maxwell

grinned. 'I'm coming back tonight, after we see this convoy to the base, and joining the Colonel.'

'In for the kill,' Fletcher said.

'Sure, wouldn't miss it. Care to come?'

'Certainly,' Fletcher said.

Maxwell threw away his half-smoked cigarette and switched on the ignition. He was a lot more relaxed than he had been before. Almost bubbling with enthusiasm.

'We'll soon clear the formalities and get the trucks through,' he said, and turned and waved at a figure at one of the windows.

They left the camp by another track which bypassed the town, and crossed the river at an old bailey bridge and ran up to the post. At the post a group of Americans were talking to a Turkish officer. One of them was Young. When he saw Fletcher, he waved and lumbered over to him.

'Well, I'm dog-garned!' he drawled in his lazy accent. 'If it isn't Fettos. You came after all.'

Fletcher accepted the handshake and got out of the jeep. In the background he saw three fresh-faced students standing around their jeep, watching them. He also saw Maxwell and the Turkish officer were getting together.

'Where's your camera?' Young asked.

'I left in rather a hurry this morning,' Fletcher explained.

'David been rushing you, eh?'

'Something like that,' Fletcher replied and changed the subject. 'I believe you phoned me at my office in Athens.'

'That's correct,' Young said without hesitation. 'We were visiting one of our schemes, and Dr Bradshaw thought it might interest you.'

Dr Bradshaw! Fletcher wondered at his interest.

'But you'll see more out here,' Young added. 'When we get these trucks delivered, I'll show you some of the sights.'

'Thanks,' Fletcher said. 'That'll be great.'

Maxwell joined them.

'The Lieutenant wants to inspect the trucks,' he said seriously. 'Greg, will you take him around the first four, and I'll pick up the rest with the Sergeant.'

'Sure,' Young drawled, 'but why the interest? Hell! we've come through here so many times, those trucks could find their own way to the base.'

But Fletcher knew what they were looking for. He caught Maxwell's eye and Maxwell moved his head, frantically, indicating that Fletcher should join Young. They crossed over the border and joined the Lieutenant and his Sergeant. The Iraqui soldiers stood by, silently watching.

The trucks were square-nosed, ugly-looking vehicles, which could be driven any-

where. The first four were driverless, waiting for the four Americans to take them over, but the rear four vehicles all had native drivers, who stood patiently alongside their cabs waiting for the formalities to be cleared.

Maxwell and the Sergeant went to the rear of the convoy, the Lieutenant strolled casually around the first truck, and Young showed his displeasure of the inspection by sitting in the cab of his vehicle and lighting a cigarette. Fletcher kept close to the Lieutenant. It wasn't a thorough search, but they saw sufficient to assure him that it was agricultural implements and fertilizers in the trucks and not weapons. When they met Maxwell he shook his head and muttered, 'Medical stuff.'

The Lieutenant suggested they returned to his hut to complete the formalities. En route he gave Young the go-ahead. Within a matter of seconds all the trucks had drivers and were moving into the town, leaving a trail of sand dust behind them. By the time Maxwell had signed the necessary papers, the leading vehicles could be seen in the distance, starting their climb out of the valley.

Maxwell took a last look at the mountains on the Turkish border before leaving the control point.

'Seems peaceful enough,' he sighed. 'We'll see what tomorrow brings.'

They drove through the town and passed small groups of Kurds and Turkish soldiers standing around the open stalls. Some of them would be Kaddir's men, Fletcher thought, and felt a little uneasy. Knowing Kaddir as he did he had a feeling it wasn't going to be so straightforward as Maxwell imagined. Kaddir would be keeping a close watch on the army, especially with Fletcher on the loose. It worried him.

They soon caught up with the convoy. The native drivers were making heavy weather of the climb, and even on the descending slope they drove their vehicles very slowly. Only Young and his compatriots appeared to handle their trucks with confidence. Gradually the distance between the American and native drivers increased. Fletcher could imagine the Americans' eagerness to show their skill over the locals, and get their vehicles back to the base well before the over-cautious tail-enders. But as the afternoon wore on and the sun disappeared behind the peaks, and the valley from which Fletcher and Reba had joined the road, loomed up in front of them, Fletcher became suspicious. Were the four native drivers working to rule on purpose? The valley had a flat, baked dry bed, with short, yellow grass, close to the river. A vehicle such as those trucks could travel far into the valley before darkness. And once darkness came the trucks could be

stripped bare in minutes, and the supplies quickly transported over the passes to Kaddir's base. That was if the drivers were driving slowly intentionally. He glanced across at Maxwell. He was leaning back in the seat casually steering the jeep with one hand. He appeared unperturbed at the speed of the convoy. Fletcher said nothing and waited.

As they neared the closest point to where a truck would leave the road to enter the valley, Fletcher could feel the excitement mounting in his body. He could be wrong, but if he was correct...! My God! he thought, if he was right!

The convoy came to a halt and he got his answer!

The first truck bounced its way over the uneven ground, disturbing a flock of wild fowl which screeched their way into the sky. Inside the jeep the two men sat silently looking at each other, Fletcher with a rather sad, disappointed expression on his face, and Maxwell a faint smile on his lips. In Maxwell's hand was his short, stubby revolver, with the hair trigger, and the muzzle pointing at Fletcher.

So this was where the final scene was to be enacted, Fletcher thought. On a rough, dusty track, in the heart of the mountains. Far away from his normal territory. Far away from help.

'How long have you known?' Maxwell

asked quietly.

Fletcher saw the second vehicle leave the track and swirl the loose, yellow sand, into a cloud of dust.

'For certain, two minutes ago,' he sighed, 'but I think I suspected it from the beginning.'

'How did you figure that?' Maxwell asked.

Fletcher suddenly felt deflated like a person discovering that his friend was not a true friend, but someone who had really despised him. The world was filled with deceit. There was no such thing as trust any more.

'I think I had my doubts from the moment Timovsky was murdered,' he said. 'He puzzled me. To begin with, I could never understand why you didn't open up your contact with him again when he returned to Turkey. Why you passed him over to British Intelligence instead. Now I know why. You were afraid he already suspected you were working for them. And there was only two possible reasons for his murder. Either the K.G.B. internal security caught up with him, or someone gave them the tip off. Everyone was quick to give the credit to the K.G.B., but I had my doubts. They would never have let him loose in Istanbul. He would have been taken back for treatment. So it looked as if they had been warned, and there weren't many who knew.'

'You are a shrewd man,' Maxwell said

grimly, 'but not shrewd enough or else you would not be sitting here.'

'True,' Fletcher agreed. 'It also puzzled me how Kaddir was allowed to run his training camp without you knowing. I had my suspicions, but I couldn't being myself to believe them.'

The third vehicle moved into the yellow cloud of dust. 'You must have had a few anxious moments,' Fletcher said baiting him. 'You killed Ali to keep his mouth shut and you also tried to kill me.'

'Yes, I tried to get you killed,' Maxwell said flatly without any sign of remorse.

'Why? Was I getting too close to you?'

'Something like that,' Maxwell replied. 'I'm glad I didn't succeed.' He laughed. 'You have to hand it to them, Fletcher, they can think up the schemes.'

'And what's this scheme about?' Fletcher asked. 'Tell me.'

Maxwell looked pleased with himself. 'You and I organized this little lot,' he said, waving at the three trucks moving away from them. The fourth was about to join them. 'A combined effort of American and British Intelligence. Together we bring the stuff in. There are plenty of witnesses. And,' he chuckled, 'we got it from an Englishman who operates a gun-smuggling syndicate.'

'Which you knew about,' Fletcher said.

'Let us say I had strong suspicions. I have

197

had my eye on Wilson for a while.'

It was damning evidence, Fletcher thought. Even if the British and American Intelligence could prove they were innocent, they were going to be made to look pretty stupid. No wonder Kaddir hadn't bothered to hunt Fletcher out. There had been no need to. Not with Maxwell working for them. As for Maxwell's plans with Colonel Sheriff, they had been a pure figment of Maxwell's imagination. The only thing the Turks would recall was that he and Maxwell had brought the convoy into Turkey.

'Why?' he asked, but again knew the answer.

'As the man said,' Maxwell replied lightly, 'they lost face over the Arab-Israeli war. They had to restore their image. Even if our Governments manage to persuade the world that they were taken for a ride, they are going to look pretty stupid, and that's important in this part of the world.'

Fletcher was only too well aware of the fact. It was his sole occupation, keeping one jump ahead of the Russians. Who ever lost face, lost influence with the Arab world – they were like that.

'Also,' Maxwell added, 'these mountains are of great strategic importance.' He didn't enlarge upon his statement, there was no need to. Fletcher knew only too well their importance.

As the fourth vehicle bounced its way off the road on to the hard clay, Fletcher had to admit that on this occasion it looked as if their elaborate scheme was going to pay dividends. He still had this in mind when he saw a figure leap from the rear of the last truck! His spirits soared and he looked at Maxwell, but the American was watching him and not the truck. From the corner of his eye Fletcher saw the figure dart behind a nearby boulder. It had looked like Lipman, but he wasn't certain. He quickly got Maxwell talking again.

'Do you really think Kaddir is going to be any match for the Turks?' he asked. 'Even with ammunition.'

The American gave a superior smile.

'Don't underestimate him,' he said. 'That's what we did in Cuba and Vietnam, and see what happened. In these mountains he can hold his own. Oh! the Turks will raze his settlement to the ground and kill a few, but that will help his cause. Before long the whole region will be ablaze from the Black Sea to Afghanistan.'

'Those supplies won't last him a month,' Fletcher scoffed.

'Two months,' Maxwell corrected him. 'He has all the weapons. We are just supplying him with the ammunition. He already has some.'

'And after two months?' Fletcher said.

'By that time there will be a strong body of world opinion on his side,' Maxwell said in his Chicago accent. 'The pitch has been prepared. After all, it is their third attempt to get independence. Even Britain and America might be persuaded to give it favourable consideration in exchange for some favour.'

'Blackmail you mean,' Fletcher retorted.

'Call it what you will,' Maxwell said, 'but whatever happens the Communists can't lose.'

No, Fletcher thought, they couldn't. They thrived on trouble of any kind.

'The Russians might even intervene,' Maxwell added. 'After all it is on their border.'

Fletcher saw the figure move to behind another boulder closer to them – it was Lipman!

'And what about me?' he asked.

'That depends upon you and them,' Maxwell said. 'But first you are going to drive us into that valley.'

Maxwell moved out of the jeep and stood facing Fletcher, his gun in his hand.

'Why?' Fletcher asked seriously, trying to delay him. 'Why did you do it?'

Maxwell's face hardened.

'Because I'm sick of the whole bloody business,' he snapped. 'Sick of killing, lying, cheating, stealing.' His eyes narrowed and his face flushed up. 'For twenty-five years I have fought their filthy war. Living with it night and day, scheming for them, just like you are now. I know what's going through your mind, Fletcher. How can I stop them? How can I save them? You're a fool. They don't deserve saving. They are not so pure and white as you imagine.'

'Are the Communists any better?' Fletcher retorted hotly. 'Are they any purer?'

'Are they any worse?' Maxwell asked angrily.

'Yes, they are,' Fletcher fumed. 'They exist on fear.'

'Fear! My God, Fletcher, don't you think we do? Only our fear is the fear of losing the power of the almighty dollar.'

His eyes were blazing. 'There is more to life than money, more than even fighting for a cause. I am going to find it. I am opting out. I am finished. They can sort out their own bloody business without me.'

'But you still haven't told me why?' Fletcher shouted at him. 'You could have opted out without turning traitor.'

'You think so?' Maxwell scoffed. 'You've been out here too long, Fletcher. You're blind to what is going on. Everything has a price and this is my price. After that they can all go to hell.'

'You're the one that's blind,' Fletcher shouted. 'Do you think they will leave you alone? Do you honestly think you are going to be able to put your feet up and relax?

They'll bleed you to death.'

Maxwell's face hardened, the lines under his eyes became more accentuated. Suddenly he looked an old man. He was tired, Fletcher thought, and sick. But the gun looked steady in his hand and was still pointing at Fletcher.

'You don't understand,' Maxwell said grimly. 'There was no alternative, it was too late. I want something out of life that's worthwhile. You are still wet around the collar. One day you will realize why I am doing this, but I haven't got time to convince you now. Get into the driving seat and when I tell you, start the engine and follow those trucks. I don't want to kill you, but don't try me. I'm not going to lose out at this stage.'

He meant what he had said. Fletcher slowly shuffled into the driver's seat. As he did so he looked for Lipman and saw him move from behind the rock. So did Maxwell! Crack! crack! Two shots rang out. One from Maxwell, the other from Lipman.

Another crack! and a spurt of sand jumped up at Maxwell's feet. Maxwell fired again and Fletcher sprang at him. He hit him square on. Together they rolled over onto the ground. Fletcher clung to him and pulled him over. The revolver came away from his hand. Desperately Fletcher lashed out with his fists. Maxwell broke loose and scrambled for the revolver, but Fletcher brought him down and held him back. As he swung him around he kicked the weapon down a small embankment. But he couldn't hold him. Maxwell stood up. Crack! a whining bullet embedded itself in Maxwell's shoulder, sending him reeling to the ground. Slowly the American staggered to his feet again, a pained expression on his face. Fletcher scurried down the slope to get the weapon. From the corner of his eye he saw Lipman taking careful aim.

'No!' Fletcher cried. 'No!'

But Lipman ignored him. Crack! crack! two quick shots rang out. Fletcher turned to Maxwell. He was lying face down on the ground. Fletcher rushed over to him, but even as he knelt down, he knew he was too late. He gently turned over the American's body and saw the mutilated eye where one of the bullets had entered his skull. Maxwell's war was over. He had got off his treadmill.

Slowly Fletcher felt the anger of the waste grip his body. There had been no need to kill Maxwell. Lipman must have seen that he had no gun in his hand. It had been cold-blooded murder.

The American walked towards him, replacing his revolver in his inside pocket. His lean, dark face looked even meaner. The resentment swelled inside Fletcher.

Lipman came up to him.

'That's one the Commies won't get,' he

said, and then Fletcher hit him full and square on the jaw.

'You bloody murderer!' he yelled. The American sagged at the knees. Fletcher held him up and hit him again. 'Bloody murderer!'

As the American collapsed to the ground, Fletcher saw the nose of an army scout car appear over the rise of the hill. At the same instant came a thunderous roar as three screaming jets zoomed overhead. Everything seemed to be happening at once. One minute there had only been Fletcher and Lipman, the next they were surrounded by units of the Turkish Army and Air Force. The jets screamed up the valley and soared into the sky. They were fighters. They made a wide circle and came in again, but this time they were heading for the four trucks moving into the gorge. Again the 'planes zoomed overhead, at the same time releasing a burst of machine-gun fire which riddled the earth behind the trucks. In a matter of seconds it was all over. Four blinding flashes followed by a thunderous roar as parts of the vehicles were flung into the sky. The aircraft flew away leaving a trail of black smoke hanging over the gorge.

Fletcher turned and saw Lipman staggering to his feet. He felt no remorse. He was still sickened by the unnecessary killing.

From another scout car, he saw the bulky,

white-suited figure of Spencer emerge, but he didn't go over to him. He had had enough.

Spencer stood mopping his perspiring brow, sizing up the situation. He puffed his way over to Fletcher.

'Thank God, you're all right,' he panted. 'You've done a good job.'

'I'm glad you think so,' Fletcher snapped. 'That makes everything just right.'

'Steady,' Spencer growled. 'What's biting you, Maxwell?'

'Yes, Maxwell,' Fletcher fumed. 'Did that bloody murderer have to kill him?'

Spencer gripped his arm.

'Come on, let's have a stroll,' he said and wiped the back of his neck. He shuffled his way along the track, gently pushing Fletcher with his hand. They walked about a hundred yards in silence, before Spencer spoke.

'Maxwell didn't work alone,' he said quietly. 'He had an accomplice. Whoever it was, is still at the base. Every major leak coincided with a visit by Maxwell to the Peace Corps base at Kiran, or to wherever their inspection team was located. Maxwell wasn't the link man with the Soviets. Someone was operating a radio for them. Probably from the base to a listening post in these mountains. Part of a relay into the Soviet Union. Who is it, Stephen?'

Fletcher stopped in his tracks and laughed.

'Doesn't that bastard know?' he asked incredulously. 'Is he so trigger-happy that he has to kill him before using him?'

'We have a shrewd idea. I want you to confirm it.'

They continued with their walk. Why had Maxwell done it? Fletcher wondered. It hadn't been because of their cause. It hadn't been for money. What else would drive a man to such extremes? What was Maxwell searching for? Peace? Happiness. Contentment? Love?

'Maxwell didn't do it because of the cause,' he said quietly, 'or for money.'

'What's left?'

Fletcher didn't tell him. Instead he asked, 'Who do you suspect?'

'Dr Marsh,' Spencer growled. 'About twelve months ago, Maxwell was ordered to assess her as a security risk. She has a history of Communist sympathies. He gave her the all clear.'

It was the final confirmation. The last piece of the jigsaw. He had the whole picture now, there was no doubt in his mind.

'He did it because of her,' he sighed. 'For love.'

Spencer looked up sharply, frowned, and headed back towards the scout cars.

'For the first time in his life,' Fletcher said, 'Maxwell had found love. He was looking for a normal, quiet, peaceful life. To get married and raise a family. My God! Was that too much to ask for?'

Spencer waved to a Turkish officer who returned his signal. Almost instantly a scout car drove past them in the direction of the base camp.

'Just keep that gun-happy monster away from her, that's all I ask,' Fletcher said hotly.

Spencer stopped in his tracks.

'I'm going to prove to you that Maxwell did have to die,' he said. 'For his own sake. There was no love on her side.'

Fletcher looked at him. He had to be wrong, he thought, he had to be.

'Get the jeep and take me to the base,' Spencer ordered.

Chapter Nine

The base camp at Kiran had a stunned air about it. Small groups of sun-tanned Americans stood watching the Turkish soldiers who had suddenly taken over their camp.

Fletcher and Spencer were directed to the administration block and escorted to one of the rooms by a Turkish soldier. Inside was the officer from the scout car and two civilians, whom Fletcher recognized as members of Turkish Security. They were examining a radio and some charred pieces of paper. Spencer went up to them and engaged them in conversation. Fletcher stood back and waited. A soldier entered the room and emptied a suitcase of clothing on to the table. One of the civilians started rummaging through the articles. The other handed Spencer a document. Spencer turned to Fletcher.

'She's in there,' he said, indicating an adjoining room. 'Read this, it might help to explain why.' He handed Fletcher the document that he had been given by the Security Officer. It was a photostatic copy of a report made on Carol Marsh by the C.I.A. Fletcher frowned. He didn't question either the guilt of Carol Marsh, or the thoroughness of the C.I.A. What was Spencer driving at? What did he want him to read. He didn't have to look far. On the front sheet, which listed Carol Marsh's personal details, three words had been underlined. Three words which were a probable explanation for the path she had chosen to take – 'of coloured ancestry'. Three words, which in certain societies, could have a damning effect.

The rest of the report was a chronological history of her life and the extent of her Communist sympathies. Her interest in Communism had started at College and although there was no proof of her being an active member of the party, there was evidence that she had supported a number of neo-Communist movements after leaving College, and had attended several Communist-sponsored meetings. Her medical career was chequered and one of constant movement, and Fletcher wondered if this was anything to do with her background.

He handed the report back to Spencer.

'Do you still want to speak to her?' Spencer asked.

'Yes,' Fletcher said firmly. He had read nothing which had made Maxwell's killing any more palatable.

Spencer stood aside and Fletcher went into the adjoining room. A Turkish soldier looked at him with surprise, but the khaki-clad figure of Carol Marsh stood with her back to the door, staring out of the window. Fletcher waved the soldier out of the room.

'I am sorry about Maxwell,' Fletcher said gently, when they were alone.

She turned at the sound of his voice and looked at him, defiantly.

'What about him?' she asked coolly.

Fletcher took a deep breath. He thought she had been told.

'He is dead,' he said softly.

Her face didn't soften.

'What am I supposed to say?' she asked in the same abrupt manner.

Fletcher looked at her, stunned.

'You could at least say you are sorry,' he snapped.

'All right. I am sorry. Are you satisfied?'

'Of all the callous bitches,' Fletcher fumed.

'Come, Mr Fettos,' she said icily. 'You are tarnishing your image. You are the modern knight in shining armour. The one who always wins through and is courteous and polite to his opponents, especially when they are women.'

'And you are the cold, frigid Communist?'

'There now, we understand each other.'

So that's what Spencer had wanted him to see. A frigid woman, dedicated to a cause, who had used Maxwell. But he still wouldn't believe it.

'No, we don't,' he snapped, 'because I knew

David Maxwell. He was no Communist, no traitor. He wasn't going to throw everything to one side for an iceberg. Maxwell was in love with you, so you must have something which lurks beneath that crust.'

'Don't be a fool,' she retorted hotly. 'Maxwell was in love with love. He was like a boy who had never been weaned,' she laughed contemptuously. 'Maxwell could have been in love with a thousand other women.'

'You know that's not true,' Fletcher retorted. 'If Maxwell had wanted a woman, he need only have snapped his fingers. No, Maxwell was in love with you all right.'

'What makes you so sure?' she sneered.

'Because I spoke to him before he died. I know why he was doing it. He wanted something out of life that he had never wanted before. Maxwell wanted marriage and a family.'

'Marriage!'

'Yes, damn you, marriage. Despite everything.'

'Despite my background?' she asked mockingly.

'Damn your background,' Fletcher fumed. 'For God's sake get the monkey off your back. The world's changing. Out here colour is only a question of degree. Maxwell wasn't concerned with colour.'

Fletcher breathed heavily and waited for her to snap back at him. But she didn't. She abruptly turned her head away from him, and stared out of the window.

The room suddenly went quiet, very quiet. Fletcher waited.

'You are right,' she said finally. 'It is different out here, but it was too late.' There was a sadness in her voice.

Too late! Maxwell had said the same, Fletcher thought. Too late, because she was already in their grasp, already committed to them.

'Maxwell did want to marry you?' Fletcher asked.

'Yes,' she sighed, still with her back to him. 'He wasn't the first American to ask me,' she added, 'but he was the first one who was prepared to go through with it.' She laughed. 'The fact that I have a coloured background didn't matter to him.'

She turned and looked at him. Fletcher couldn't see her face, it was in the shadow, but he knew the fire had gone out of her. She was the Carol Marsh he had met before.

'What about you?' she asked. 'Would it have mattered to you?'

Fletcher didn't hesitate in answering.

'Not if I loved anyone as much as Maxwell must have loved you,' he said.

She didn't reply. She stood in the shadow, far away in thought.

'Were you going to marry him?' Fletcher asked.

He had to know.

The question jolted her. She turned her back on him again.

'Go away!' she cried. 'Leave me alone!'

Fletcher stood his ground.

'Leave me alone!' she cried again. 'Please.'

As Fletcher went to the door she started to sob. Gently at first and then uncontrollably. Fletcher had got his answer.

'There will be other times, and other Maxwells,' he said. He didn't know whether she heard him. He hoped she had.

The soldier re-entered the room and Fletcher joined Spencer. He had his back to Fletcher, but he turned to face him.

'Well?' he asked gruffly.

'He didn't have to die,' Fletcher said.

Spencer shrugged. 'You can't win them all,' he said and turned his back on him again.

Fletcher suddenly felt the need for some fresh air.

The first rays of the morning sun shone through the metal grille onto the dark green wall of the room, picking out its rough, chipped surface.

Fletcher and Spencer sat silently contemplating all that had been said, and drinking the last of the bottle which Spencer always managed to save for such occasions. They had talked all through the night, examining all that had taken place from every angle, so that Spencer could send his report to the Foreign Office.

They had learned to add another danger to the long list of reasons why a person could defect – love! If it was felt strong enough, it was capable of distorting a person's normal comprehension. Maxwell had fallen into this trap with Carol Marsh, and it was ironical that their introduction and constant companionship had been ordered by the State Department in Washington. Carol Marsh's interest in Communism had not been forgotten when she had come East with the Corps. When she had earned the right to a position of more authority, Maxwell had been detailed to keep her under surveillance, and to assess her as a security risk. In doing so he had become so emotionally involved that he was prepared to make any sacrifice to protect her and become part of her life. But Carol Marsh alone was not to blame. Maxwell had had his belly full, and for that the men behind the scenes were responsible. They had sapped him of his vitality and loyalty.

As for Carol Marsh – she had turned traitor to hit back at a society which had scorned her because of the colour of her ancestors. The full facts of her work had not yet come to light, but after she recovered from her present nervous collapse, they would get the information. Whether or not she had operated in the States was questionable but Spencer felt certain that she had been in league with the Communists when she was accepted for the Corps. Besides operating her own radio link from her quarters in the base camp, she would also have contacts in the various cities she had visited, so that she could pass on the information.

The Turks had taken over the responsibility of Kaddir and despatched a company of paratroopers to his settlement. But Fletcher was sceptical about his capture, and equally doubtful whether they had heard the last of him. If the Turks and their bordering countries were wise, they would take heed of the warning. If they didn't, Kaddir, or someone like him, would emerge, and it would all start again.

The West had achieved a victory. They had beaten the Russians at their own game. Without Kaddir, his network of agents would collapse, and the West now knew what they were looking for. The K.G.B. was going to have to think again. One of the reasons why the K.G.B. had failed was because they had underestimated their opposition. The British Intelligence was thin on the ground, but their contacts were numerous and reliable. Nico's men had proved that. Spencer had soon learned of Fletcher's disappearance after visiting the villa. Spencer had also been given sufficient information about the other visitor to the villa for him to trace his identity to Wilson. He had immediately laid out an extensive network of local agents and picked up Fletcher's movements as he was being taken by car and boat to a Greek island, and flown to a landing strip close to the border of Turkey and Iraq. Spencer had suspected that Fletcher was under drugs, but couldn't get close enough to verify without making them suspicious. If he had interfered Fletcher could have come to more harm, and they would never have seen the final playoff. As it was, Spencer stepped back, and sent out a call to reliable Turkish and pro-Western agents in the Eastern provinces. The plane had landed in Iraq and Fletcher's move into the mountains had been watched from a distance. By now Spencer had followed up Fletcher's request to chase up Washington for news about Young and Marlow. An immediate reply from Washington to the effect that there was no query in the pipeline about those two men put Spencer on to Maxwell. Spencer went to the Ambassador and at that level the line between Athens and Washington hummed with activity. Washington told them of their own suspicions about Maxwell's effectiveness and that Lipman, another C.I.A. man, was working independent of Maxwell.

Spencer knew of Fletcher's means of contacting Maxwell and got the Turkish

Security to work on the cobbler. The Turk had no alternative, but to co-operate, and had informed them when Fletcher had turned up. Spencer and Lipman had got together and exchanged notes. When Lipman had told him of the shipment Wilson had arranged for the supply of the stores to the base at Kiran, Spencer had put two and two together and he and Lipman had moved to Zamdi to await developments. Unknown to the Kurds, the convoy was observed from a distance and the switch of stores, which was made shortly after it left Baghdad, was dutifully reported to Spencer. In Zamdi, Lipman got himself aboard the rear vehicle as it was passing through the town and the Turkish Air Force 'planes ordered to stand by. Fletcher's imagination had not played tricks on him when he thought he had seen a familiar back in the Colonel's office. It had been Spencer. But Spencer had not expected Maxwell to delay the convoy any longer by spending fifteen purposeless minutes with the Turkish Commander. It had nearly resulted in a last-minute give away. Maxwell had to be caught in the act. There had to be no doubt of his guilt, and there had to be no means of bad publicity afterwards! If Maxwell was guilty he had to pay the price. Russia was not going to be allowed to make capital out of it. Carol Marsh was a different case. She was a Soviet spy – Maxwell was a C.I.A. man who had defected.

The two men sat silently playing with their glasses, each to their own thoughts.

It was Spencer who spoke first.

'Maxwell was wrong on two accounts,' he said in a more gentle tone than he normally used.

Fletcher looked at him over his glass. Spencer had his head bent as if studying the pitted surface of the wooden table. Fletcher contemplated his glass again.

'Only two?' he asked.

'Yes, only two. He got too emotionally involved in his work. It became a personal battle for him. For far too long he fought them all single-handed. It ate him up. He was on a treadmill which never stopped.' He paused and took a drink. 'Until eventually the treadmill snapped.' He raised his sagging head to look at Fletcher. 'I don't want you to end up like Maxwell,' he said pointedly. 'It can easily happen.'

Fletcher grunted. It was not the first time Spencer had talked to him in such a manner. There was a bond between the two men which went further than their business relationship. Spencer had often expressed his concern at the way Fletcher became engrossed in his work. But Fletcher knew no other way to keep on top – and to keep alive. He didn't feel like arguing his case with

Spencer again. The warm, cigar-roasted air was beginning to tire him. He had had enough.

But not Spencer.

'The second thing, Stephen, was that Maxwell thought he was entitled to happiness,' he said, 'but no one is entitled to anything.' This was a topic Spencer had never broached before. Fletcher wasn't sure he wanted him to continue.

'Maxwell thought he was entitled to happiness as a right.' Spencer pursued his point. 'There are no rights!' he said, 'only opportunities, and you have to grasp them while you can. You can't demand them afterwards like Maxwell.'

Spencer sagged back in his chair. His sermon was over. But his remarks had not fallen on barren ground. Fletcher realized the wisdom of them. He also became acutely aware that the only thing he really wanted to do at that very moment was to see Reba again. Even the thought of her sent a wave of excitement through his body.

'I think I might stay behind for a while,' he said, looking at the drink in his glass, 'to see what develops.'

Spencer yawned.

'I rather thought you would,' he said in a matter of fact tone.

Fletcher smiled and wondered whether he had really thought of it himself, or had

Spencer put the thought in his mind.

'When are you leaving?' Fletcher asked.

'Afternoon 'plane from Hakkari for Ankara,' Spencer said. 'Here is your passport and enough money to see you by for a while.' He threw a Greek passport and a roll of money onto the table. 'I'll expect you back in two weeks.' He struggled to his feet. 'I think I'll get some rest,' he said, stretching himself.

Fletcher placed the passport and money in his pocket and ran his hand over his chin. He would need a shave.

'You know, Stephen,' Spencer said with a smile, 'my wife thinks I am at the Royal in Rhodes for a few days rest.' He looked around the spartan room which the Turks had placed at their disposal and gave a deep, rumbling laugh. 'Or so she tells me,' he added as a sudden afterthought, and trudged wearily out of the room.

As Fletcher crossed the old wooden bridge he could see the farm beyond the spur of the hill. Two small, white buildings, sparkled in the morning sunrise. Behind him was the neat rows of huts of the camp and the untidy, flat-roofed buildings of the town, with the first smoke of the day starting to curl into the sky.

It was peaceful in the valley and even the sheep were respecting the sanctity of the early morning.

Fletcher inhaled the sweet, fresh, dewy air, and hurried towards the two buildings, but long before he got there he saw Reba. She was standing a short distance away from the buildings as if she was waiting for him…

The publishers hope that this book has given you enjoyable reading. Large Print Books are especially designed to be as easy to see and hold as possible. If you wish a complete list of our books please ask at your local library or write directly to:

Magna Large Print Books
Magna House, Long Preston,
Skipton, North Yorkshire.
BD23 4ND